THE 11TH HOUR MOTEL

A THRILLER

BEAU SAVAGE

GRIM HEART
PUBLISHING

THE 11TH HOUR MOTEL

MISSY

$\mathcal{N}$ights like these. A night like this. I can't help being reminded of you, always. But I suppose that's nothing new. When am I not thinking of you? I can scarcely recall the last moment I wasn't. Something about tonight just has me remembering differently, I guess.

Storms will do that.

I'm sitting in our living room watching a movie I've watched too many times already—and will probably go on to watch many more times even still—as the storm picks up, blowing hard against the house so that its skeleton groans and creaks as the wind whips around the gutters outside. I've already had to turn up the volume twice because the storm just keeps getting stronger. Louder.

Nights like these.

I pause my movie as the next gust rattles the house's bones, then pause in my chair as the handsome actor frozen on the television screen reminds me of you that much more. More than usual. It hurts, how much he reminds me of you, but that's probably why I've watched this movie so many times now that I've lost count. No, not *probably.* That's one-hundred percent why. I can't lie to myself about that. I've watched it so many times that I could recite the actors' lines before they do.

Some people would think me mighty strange for the repetition I've invited into my life these days, just to keep you close to me. But of course, everyone believes what they don't understand to be strange. Not many people can understand what we had, or what it's like to let something so powerful go.

Not many people know loss like I do.

Finally I stand up out of my chair and pace into the hall-way, into the front entryway—or the lobby, as I like to call it. The phone on the wall behind the counter hasn't rung for hours. No one will call tonight. Not on a night like this.

I approach the front door, where I can hear the wind sweeping over the house and into the darkness that lies beyond our property. I know the cold that awaits me outside, but I pull the door open anyway, enough to ding the bell over my head. An icy plume of powder immedi-ately swirls through the gap, peppering my face.

You used to love storms like this. *Dangerous.* Whether it was rain or snow or just a great deal of dust, you always reveled in the power of it. The violence of it. And I suppose I loved them, too. I suppose I still do, even if they're tainted now with this longing I can't shake. It's difficult to be reminded of something I want so badly but will never have again—an addiction I'm incapable of satisfying.

Because you're gone.

Just like this storm will be gone by morning, the world in its wake less defined under a heaping helping of snow, my memory of you will fade likewise, slightly harder to recall, to imagine the shape of you smoothed over under a heaping helping of *time.*

It's all I can do to resist sinking my numb hands into our cold past and burying myself underneath alongside you.

I squint through it, the blowing snow, and fold my arms across my sweater vest as I peer into the black night, toward the snow-covered road where our towering sign casts a wide cone of red light onto the ground around it, advertising that our little motel is here, it's open, it's available, choose me, choose me, choose me! I doubt I'll be receiving any guests, however. Not on a night like this. Not in a storm like this.

Anyone driving on these deserted roads in such a storm would have to be dumb or desperate or both.

JASPER

I thrum my fingers against the steering wheel as I wait. My hands are pale as hell in the dark, in the cold, the winter bleeding through the windows faster than my car can blow heat through its vents, apparently.

Or maybe it's something else that chills me.

The city street is unmoving. I'm parked as dead-center as can be between the street lights, in as much shadow as I could find. I glance at the time again and again. It's taking longer than I'd like. *He's* taking longer than I'd like. Wyatt, the asshole. Well, he's not really an asshole. Or at least he's no more an asshole than I am. We're *both* assholes, if I'm being honest. That's why we're here, isn't it? That's why I'm waiting in this cold. That's why he's inside right now, on the third floor of this apartment building, stealing through a unit that isn't his, isn't mine, taking something that doesn't belong to either of us.

"Hurry the hell up," I whisper to myself.

The sound of my own voice is a slight comfort. Reminds me that I'm *me*. I haven't felt like *me* much these last few days. Maybe longer than that. Maybe *much* longer than that, now that I really think about it. I look into the rearview, into my own eyes, and I *recognize* them there, those eyes, but I don't recognize what's inside them.

The eyes looking back at me look scared as shit.

"Come on, Wyatt."

In and out, Wyatt said. In and out, five minutes tops. But as I look at the clock again I can see that it's been eleven minutes and he's still not stumbling through the front door and down the cement steps toward my car. Did something happen, I wonder? Has our plan been thwarted? Is he up there right now getting the ever-loving shit kicked out of him? Will I be next?

As if my fingers aren't pale enough, I grip the steering wheel and watch as my knuckles flex into a sickly color, a ghostly white. I fidget a bit, scratching at my thigh through my jeans. I twist the knob on my heater so that the air blows a little harder. I glance at the fuel gauge to remind myself that *yes*, I already stopped for gas, I've got a full tank, I'm ready, *we're* ready, if only Wyatt would hurry his ass up.

I'm not sure what would make me madder—if he gets himself caught, or if after all this time, all this planning, he emerges empty-handed. If Wyatt emerges empty-handed, I think I might drive away without him. I think I'll—

The front door opens. I sit forward in my seat, holding my breath. It's him. It's Wyatt. He comes out looking even more scared than I do, his eyes wide as can be, his mouth agape as he hurries down the cement steps, looking left and right like he's already forgotten where we parked. He spots me in the shadows and I see a puff of warm breath leave his mouth as he sighs with relief. He must have thought I left him for a moment. I notice the strap around his shoulder, the duffel bag bouncing against his hip, and I sigh a breath of relief, too.

I lean over and open his door, give it a push. He catches it, opens it wider, swings himself into the passenger seat with a soft grunt, dumping the bag onto the floor between his feet.

"Go," he says.

I go. I peel us away from the curb, slow and steady and as inconspicuous as possible. I see the first flakes of snow on the windshield as I turn the wheel hand over hand, gently taking us onto another street, out of sight of the apartment.

"Is that it?" I say, and flick my gaze to the bag between Wyatt's feet. "Looks smaller than I expected."

"First time I've ever heard those words," Wyatt says, and I catch him grinning in that moment, which tells me he's elated, he's feeling optimistic, that everything went as well as we could hope, well enough to be making dumb jokes as I start driving us toward the city's outskirts.

"That's all of it, though?" I say.

"That's all of it."

"Really? You're sure?"

"I'm sure, man. Chill the fuck out. We're good."

We're good. I can't begin to describe how *good* it feels to hear him say those words. *We're good.* I repeat it several times over in my mind, trying to convince myself, trying to savor those words because despite all the planning, I expected *something* to go wrong. Anything, really.

We're good, we're good, we're good.

I can't believe it.

"How much is it, do you think?"

"I don't know. A lot. It's all bundles, man."

"Bundles of what?"

"Hundreds. Bundles of *hundreds.* It's all of it, I told you."

The bag on the floor between his feet is a small duffel bag. I begin trying to estimate how many bundles of hundred-dollar bills could fit in that bag, trying to do the math, but I can hardly keep my thoughts straight. They're scattered. Tangled.

My inability to concentrate tells me how *not* good we actually are. A part of me is still panicking. A part of me is still afraid.

Another fat snowflake melts on the windshield right before my eyes, and I realize we're not out of this storm yet.

Not even close.

Wyatt goes quiet as we leave town. Too quiet. Maybe it's because the reality of our situation is settling over him, too, like it is me. Or maybe these icy roads are stressing him out. I know they're stressing *me* out. The snow is coming down heavier now. A lot heavier. More than I expected. These rural highways are great for going long distances undisturbed, but they're terrible in weather like this.

Fuck, I think, annoyed.

We even picked tonight because the forecasts said the storm wouldn't arrive until tomorrow morning.

As if the roads aren't perilous enough, I can't stop

taking my eyes away looking at that stupid bag on the floor between Wyatt's feet.

"Would you stop?" Wyatt says, noticing my split attention. "Keep your eyes on the damn road…"

"I know. I just…"

I just *what?* I don't even know. I still can't believe we've got it. All that money. I don't think my heart has stopped pounding since we pulled away from the curb.

Wyatt startles me with a breathy laugh, a gentle slap against my arm.

"Jazz, I'm playing with you," he says. "I know what you're thinking. I'm thinking about it, too."

"And what's that?"

"What this *means,*" he says. "I didn't start feeling it until we left town, when my nerves finally calmed down—what all this money means. *Shit.* I can't decide what I'm gonna do with it first. Or if I'll do *anything* with it at first. Might be smarter to wait a while. We'll see."

"Yeah," I say, though I'm not sure we're actually sharing the same headspace.

His comments have reminded me, though. About what it means. How much that money could change my life. *Will* change my life. I'm excited to call her tomorrow morning and tell her it's done. *Jennifer.* She'll already have her bags packed and ready to come meet me. I'll sell this junk heap as fast as I can—I'll take the first offer I get, I don't even care how much—and then we'll leave together toward our new life. Someplace far away. Someplace safe.

Someplace where it doesn't snow so much.

❄

We're well out of town when I see them behind us—a pair of headlights shining through the cold darkness.

Shit.

A vehicle appearing *behind us* in this way can only mean one thing: they're going fast. Faster than we are, at least. We've already driven miles without another soul in sight. To see those headlights appear, to see someone *gaining* on us in this storm, my mind immediately jumps to worst-case scenarios.

It's them. They know their money's gone. They know we took it. Somehow, they know where we're going.

"Jazz?" Wyatt says, craning his neck as he peers over his shoulder, behind his seat through the back windshield.

"I see them," I say.

I look at our speed. We're going slow. I don't dare go any faster on these roads. I tell myself I'm trying to be smart, driving cautiously like this, but with those headlights swelling gradually behind us I'm not so sure. Maybe I should have been going faster all this time. We'd be farther along.

"It can't be them," Wyatt says. "There's no way it's them."

"I don't know who the hell else it would be," I say, as if this world is so small, like there couldn't possibly be anyone as foolish as us to brave these roads tonight.

Except the vehicle behind us isn't merely *braving these roads.* They're going fast. Dangerously fast, no matter what vehicle they might be driving. They're on a mission, I think. They're in a hurry, either to get somewhere or…

Or to stop somebody else from getting somewhere. Somebody who stole something from them, maybe.

I'm being paranoid. I didn't sleep well last night and it's caught up with me tonight. That's all. But as we continue through the vortex of white snow in our headlights, I see the headlights behind us growing larger still, closer still, until finally I'm able to make out the vehicle itself. A truck. Not a shitty little sedan like we're in, but a full-sized pickup. Oddly that reassures me a little. Lots of people drive trucks. And plenty of truck drivers are cocky enough to drive like complete morons in this kind of weather. It really could be anyone. I'm just being paranoid, that's all.

Our car gives a little shake, a little swerve, and I have to let off the gas a bit as I clamp both my hands onto the wheel. At first I think we're sliding on ice, until I notice the heavy snowfall is now at a severe angle. The storm is picking up. We're driving right into it. As if the ice and snow on the roads weren't precarious enough, now I have to deal with the wind batting us around one strong gust at a time.

"Fuck, Jazz, I think it's them," Wyatt says, turning around in his seat every five seconds to check.

I look in my rearview again. They're coming so fast, they'll be right behind us any second now. In another moment I'll have to squint against their blazing headlights shining directly through the rear windshield, unless of course they choose to pass us, to pull into the oncoming lane and hurry on by, on their own business, business that has absolutely nothing to do with us because Wyatt and I are simply acting like scared little shits getting our undies in a tangle.

And wouldn't you know it, as the truck finally comes close enough to blind me a little with its lights, it swerves into the oncoming lane. They're passing us, whoever they are. They've got other places to be. Whatever mission they're on, we're not a part of it. I take a great deep breath as the truck's engine becomes audible in my ears as it pulls alongside us, hurriedly passing us without a thought or care in the—

"Oh fuck—"

...is all Wyatt can say before the back windows shatter. Glass sprinkles into the car. I hear the bullets punch each of our seats. It's not rapid enough to be automatic fire, but rather someone with a very quick and eager trigger finger. A stream of expletives cross my mind, cross my tongue, all at once so that I can hardly tell if I'm just thinking these words or shouting them aloud as the cold storm rushes into the car with us, fills my ears with its roaring. My back and shoulder alight with hot, burning pain—in direct contrast to the chill that licks the back of my neck through the broken windows.

I focus on the road ahead, except now the storm is so thick, so *violent*, I can hardly tell where the road even is. Everything is white and blowing and glittering in our headlights. The car bumps along uneven terrain on our right-hand side. I realize I'm drifting off the road. I try to steer us back, try to steer us away from the unknowable slopes and ditches that may or may not lie in wait just off the highway's shoulder. Only seconds have passed since the bullets started flying, but in the back of my mind I notice Wyatt's silence beside me, the way his voice so suddenly cuts off, the way his body jostles under his seatbelt as I struggle to straighten us back onto the road.

And then the truck hits us.

Its right bumper pushes against the left side of our tail. A calculated PIT maneuver. We start to slide. To spin. The steering wheel jerks right out of my hands as we hit the rough terrain hidden beneath the snow and in an instant I've lost all control. There's no getting it back. The car thumps, thrashes us sideways, and then our lefthand wheels are lifting off the ground. It happens so fast but feels like ages. We roll. Maybe four or five times across the snow. I catch brief glimpses through the windshield, brief visions of topsy-turvy snow and chunks of dirt spraying across the hood of my car. Wyatt's hand slaps me, I think, his knuckles smacking me in the eye as his rag-doll body flails in the passenger seat. We finally come to a stop but we're upside down, gently spinning along the roof of the car in the snow.

And then everything stops.

I hurt. I hurt in so many places, too many places for my mind to pinpoint any single injury. I'm just a human-shaped lump of aches and bruises and hot throbbing. I'm upside down in my seat, my seatbelt locked painfully against my shoulder and across my lap, holding me in place as all the blood in my body rushes to my head. I look left. I look right. Wyatt hangs beside me similarly and I'm startled as his eyes meet mine. He's alive. For now. A steady stream of dark blood runs down his face and into his dark hair. In the silence that follows, beneath the noise of the wind whistling through the windows, I hear Wyatt's blood pattering onto the roof's interior. His mouth opens, closes, but no words come out as he's just staring at me. Staring into my eyes. It's then I notice the hole in his throat, where the blood's pumping out in sync with his heartbeat. Again, only seconds pass and yet his eyes communicate so much.

I'm dying, he tells me. *I'm scared.*

My wits wash over me in a tingling surge of adrenaline, rinsing away the disorientation. If I don't move now, I know I'll be dead soon, too. I reach for my seatbelt and undo it with a click of the button and drop clumsily onto the roof beneath me. I turn myself over. Beside me, where Wyatt's dangling hands lay limp against the roof, I see his handgun lying still. He must have reached for it as the truck overcame us, perhaps only managing to pull it from his jacket before the bullets started to fly. I grab his gun. I search for my door's handle. It's confusing, with everything upside down like it is, but I find it, pull it, shove the door open enough to start squeezing out on my hands and knees into the snow.

I hear voices.

Looking ahead, slightly dizzy, the icy wind chapping my face, I think I see their figures approaching. They're coming from the road.

Fuck. Shit.

Using the side of the car for support, I climb onto my feet. I remain hunched over as I scurry around the end of the car, around the trunk to the opposite side where I drop to my knees in the cold wet snow. My body flares with pain. I think I got shot up a little, too.

No, I don't think *I got shot up. I got shot up.*

I just can't tell where at the moment. My injuries are broad swaths of *fire* along various parts of my body.

With the rolled-over car between myself and the road, I peek through the busted-out windows in the back and see them coming. Two figures, coming to survey the aftermath. Through the cold flurry, I can see the light of their truck's headlights shining behind them from the side of the road, framing them against a backdrop of dazzling snow.

I glance to the front passenger window beside me, where Wyatt's body hangs limp in his seatbelt. Poor fucker.

Then I see the duffel bag. It sits in the snow just outside his window. Right next to me.

As our two assailants come closer through the blinding flurry, I take aim through the rear windows. My breaths are shallow. Shaky. *I'm* shaky. I don't have another second to spare. I pull the trigger three times. Three gunshots pop off loudly in my already ringing ears. The figures freeze, stunned. I add a fourth pull of the trigger on a whim. One of the figures drops into the snow, their hands instantly wrapping their leg where my lucky aim has struck home. The second figure reacts at last, darts out of the way, diving into the snow and out of my line of sight.

That's fine. That's all I really needed—to distract them with fear.

I scramble toward the bag of money, throw the strap over my shoulder. I get standing as I push away from the car, deeper into the field, deeper into the blowing snow where I hope I might vanish like a ghost.

If only for a moment.

QUENTIN

*T*he idiots I have to deal with.

It shouldn't come as any surprise in my line of work, and yet I'm still routinely stunned by it—the unadulterated *idiocy*.

The problem is that I'm surrounded by opportunists. People looking for fast, easy money. Crime and shortsightedness—name a more iconic duo. It's a daunting enterprise, after all, making something of yourself the *'right'* way. Breaking the shackles of your economic class the right way, the legal way—the *'moral'* way—requires years of planning, discipline, and enough forward momentum to launch you into the Winds of Luck that may or may not carry you very far. And that's the scariest part. The simple fact that nothing is guaranteed. That you can do everything *correctly* and still fail is a reality too frightening for some. More frightening, even, than the potential consequences of taking a shortcut or two...

Crime pays, and that's a fact.

The downside is that the health insurance plans are terrible. Fatal, even.

It wasn't five minutes after Wyatt fled Erik's apartment that I was notified. Him and that golden-retriever-brained buddy of his.

Jasper.

I actually always kind of liked him, in the same way anybody likes a golden retriever. They're dumb, adorable, friendly, unwaveringly loyal… or at least they're supposed to be. It appears this one has been taught to bite. I'm almost sorry to have to put him down.

Not ten minutes after receiving the call, Allen and I are already buckled in and hitting the road. Jasper and Wyatt have a fifteen minute head start. No big deal. The roads are shit, but luckily we're taking one of the boss' trucks, and luckier still we know exactly where they're headed thanks to a helpful tip from another of Wyatt's so-called buddies who probably expects a reward for his loyalty. More likely he'll face punishment for not coming forward sooner. Oh well.

The idiots I have to deal with, am I right?

The snow is really coming down. It's thick enough that it takes me a good moment or two before I realize I see their glowing taillights in the distance, blooming through the slanted flurry.

"Get ready," I tell Allen, who startles in the passenger seat because he was dozing off.

"Is that them?" he says, shifting around as he gathers his senses again.

"That's them."

"How we wanna do this?"

I sigh. There are a few ways we can do this, obviously. Erik prefers we keep things quiet, discreet, under the radar. Most days I'm of the same mind, but in certain circumstances discretion only serves to waste one's time. Sometimes ripping the bandage off is the best route for everyone.

Wyatt and Jasper have already wasted enough of my time tonight, and I'm not in the mood to take things slowly.

"Get ready to take some cheap shots," I say, pressing the gas pedal a little harder. "I'll get into position."

Their taillights swell before us as we gain speed, closing the distance. Although this truck is more than capable, I still feel the ice under the tires—our traction holding solid for the most part, with some *interesting* catches now and again.

As the shape of the sedan materializes through the overwhelming red glow of its taillights, I'm certain their vehicle doesn't stand a chance in weather like this. If Allen can't pick them off with a few shots, I'll help nature take its course.

Allen rolls down his window as we come up on their rear. The blustery chill of winter rushes in, nearly makes me gasp. Allen leans out of his seat, his pistol in both hands out the window, arms rested against the door as I pull us into the oncoming lane, pressing the gas a little more. The tires slip a little bit, just enough that only I notice it, the steering wheel pulling in my grasp. We pull up alongside them, my ears full of wind and the sound of tires whipping snow before Allen's gunshots flash and pop like firecrackers. The little sedan beside us swerves, drifts, swerves again. I'm careful to avoid them. For now. They're desperately trying to stay on the road. Through the visual noise of the snow and the gleam of our headlights, I make out the face behind the wheel of the sedan. It's Jasper. Both hands white-knuckled on the steering wheel, he glances our way, but those eyes of his aren't seeing a damn thing, blinded by terror.

Allen empties his magazine and the kid is still holding strong, maintaining speed, both hands glued to the wheel.

I let off the gas, losing speed, losing distance, just enough that I can jerk the wheel in their direction and give the tail of the sedan a nice little *bump*.

Nature takes its course.

I'll be honest, I'm awestruck as their vehicle slides off the road and promptly *flips*, again and again like an aluminum soup can rolling through the snow. I gently tap the brakes, coming to a stop along the shoulder.

"Shit," Allen says, craning his neck to see the wreck as their car comes to a stop in the middle of the field.

"You ready?" I ask.

Allen pops open the glovebox, where he removes a box of handgun ammunition and begins reloading his magazine.

"Let's finish this," I say, as I open my door and hop out of the truck.

No more time to waste.

I reach inside my jacket and pull my own handgun from my shoulder holster, stepping around the rear of the truck. Allen's passenger door slams shut as he comes to join me. Peering across the field, I can barely see the sedan.

Its one surviving headlight shines into the cold abyss. I roll onto my toes slightly as a gust of wind presses against my back, like the storm itself is urging me to get this over with.

We begin our approach. My boots crunch through old snow, into the dead grass and weeds buried underneath. I squint as the new snow flurries around me. The cold stings my eyes. It isn't until I'm several steps into the field that I realize the sedan is *upside down,* sitting atop its roof. Whatever shape they're in, it's not *good.*

I raise a hand as I slow my pace, signaling for Allen to slow down as well but he's not paying any attention to me. He moves past me, continuing toward the wreck.

And that's when the gunfire starts.

Three gunshots in quick succession, followed by a fourth. It's the late bloomer that drops Allen into the snow. He sits on his ass, hissing through his teeth as he pulls his leg against himself.

Idiot. Idiot. Idiot.

The gunshots surprise me, however, and it's a moment before I can get my body to react. I trudge out of the way, stomping through uneven snow piles until I lose my footing and fall to my knees. The blowing snow cuts my visibility in half. The glow of the red taillights and the single headlight is just enough to deepen the surrounding dark by contrast, so that I can hardly decipher what moves and what doesn't. Even with the wind howling in my ears, I hear Allen's pained gasping.

Idiot.

I pick myself up. I skirt around the edge of the darkness, where the car's lights don't reach, where I know I'm hidden behind the curtain of snow coming down, as well as behind the billowing powder the wind sweeps up.

If I can't see them, they can't see me.

I continue around, one careful step at a time. There are no further gunshots, not even to finish Allen off. I can't stop thinking what an idiot he is. I almost wish they would open fire again and finish what they started. At least if they did I could see precisely where they're hiding and return fire accordingly. Obviously they're taking cover behind the car. Are they injured, I wonder? I can't help feeling there's no possible way they escaped Allen's gunfire *and* the wreck unscathed.

I continue circling, staying a fair distance away in the dark, in the snow, toward the other side of the car. I can't see anything. Anyone. I move steadily closer, my gun aimed and ready. As I move in, and the shadows along the length of the car soften...

I realize no one's there.

I turn—you might even call it a flinch—toward the darkness beside me as another fresh gust of wind lifts powder into the air, blinding me. As the gust wanes, and the snow dust settles, I see no one. No one close, anyway. I move closer to the car. I bend down a little, getting a view inside.

There's someone still in the passenger seat. Dangling. Unmoving. That would be Wyatt, I think.

He must be dead.

Shit.

That means Jasper's out here somewhere. I flinch again. No denying it this time. I pivot, stepping over my own feet as I swing my gun toward the shadows behind me. Nothing but white against the black. I spin on my heel again, back to the car. I move around it once more, so that I can see Allen's pathetic figure still lying in the snow cradling himself. Our truck is still idling by the side of the road, invisible there except for the taillights and the illuminated wedge of snowfall caught in the headlights.

Suddenly those lights start to move.

"Uh, hey," I say, my voice merely a whisper as my thoughts pile up in a stunned stupor. "Hey!"

I scream as I chase around the flipped sedan, stomping my boots through the snow toward Allen, toward the road, toward our truck that's steadily rolling onward all on its own, gaining speed, the lights sinking into the dark with distance.

"*Hey!*"

I reach the road in utter futility. I even point my gun at those shrinking lights, as if I could hope to stop him from such a distance. A white plume of breath leaves my panting mouth. I lower my gun. I glance to the wreck, to Allen peering toward me confusedly from the ground, then back to the road where those crimson beads of light get smaller and smaller.

"Fuck!"

I can't believe this. I absolutely cannot fucking believe this. I turn to the open field, push a hand through my wet hair as I pace along the road's shoulder.

"Oh my God, oh my *God!*"

I slip my gun back into its holster before I can pull the trigger by accident, as my fingers involuntarily curl themselves into fists. My mind is racing.

What the hell are we supposed to do now?

Jesus Christ, this is embarrassing.

How are we going to tell Erik about this?

We *cannot* tell Erik about this.

But obviously we'll have to.

We're stranded.

I'm literally huffing and puffing along the side of the road when Allen's whiney voice calls to me from the field. I don't hear what he says. It sounds like a question. *What happened?* Something like that. That better not be what he's asking me. The idiot.

I stomp my way back through the field toward him, toward the wreck.

"Did that just happen?" Allen says. "Did they... did they really just..."

It's all I can do to resist pulling my gun from its holster again and silencing him. I pay him no mind. I continue toward the turned-over car. Another gust of wind blows powder into my face. My cheeks are numb. I pull open the passenger door and crouch there, studying the body still secured by its seatbelt.

The poor bastard is still alive.

"Oh! How you doin, Wyatt?"

I undo his seatbelt for him. He collapses onto the roof in a wheezing heap. I reach in, find an ankle, and proceed to drag him out of the car and onto his back. I drop him there alongside the car. A dark streak of blood trails him in the snow. His mouth hangs open but he seems unable to speak. I notice the gunshot wound in his throat, where most if not all the blood has come from. His eyes roll in their sockets, tracking me as I come to stand beside him. My knees pop as I crouch down again. I open my mouth to speak but realize I'm wasting my time. This man is as good as dead.

I pull my handgun from my jacket, point the barrel between Wyatt's eyes, and pull the trigger. His expression remains mostly the same, dead or alive. I re-holster my gun and climb inside the upside-down car. I check the glovebox, the backseat. I pop the trunk from the driver's side and go check to see what's fallen out. There I discover an emergency roadside kit as well as a medium travel case, but it's not the money we're looking for. I grab both anyway. I carry the emergency roadside kit against my hip and drag the travel case through the snow behind me on my way back to Allen.

"Is that it?" he says, still sprawled on his ass. "You got the money?"

"No. He made off with the money."

And our truck, I think but don't say. Again, it's too embarrassing.

"So… now what?" Allen says.

I'm about to tell him we've got a long hike back into town, but then I remember his leg. His stupid fucking leg. Once more I'm tempted to finish him off myself, put him out of his misery like an old dog. Instead I just sigh heavily and ask him:

"Can you even walk?"

LANA

I watch the white lines on the road zip underneath us, one by one by one in quick succession through the warm light of the headlights. It would be hypnotic if I wasn't so preoccupied with my own thoughts. My own drama. My own nonsense.

It's all nonsense, really.

I'm the master of it. I craft nonsense like nobody's business, all without even trying. I'm helpless to avoid it, it seems. At least that's what I tell myself.

That's what my thoughts are circling as the first snowflakes start gathering on my windshield. Nonsense.

Him.

I know he's thinking of me, too. I've been trying not to look at my phone these past few hours because I know the messages he's sent won't be anything good. Not for me. He's angry. Understandably so, after the things I've told him. The *nonsense* I've traded. That's the thing about my flavor of nonsense, is it's hardly ever harmless.

But in this case, I think he deserves it.

I *know* he deserves it.

But there's this nagging voice in my head I can't silence. Let's call it a *voice of reason.* It's telling me to forget about him, to move on, to stop stewing in my neurotic fantasies before I hurt my own feelings. I'm really good at that, too— hurting my own feelings. It comes with the territory of nonsense. The distinct lack of reason, of structure. If I say that I have a tendency to hurt other people, I'm almost always hurting myself tenfold. And this nagging voice keeps telling me to *stop, stop, stop* before I end up damaging myself in some irreparable way.

Slow down.

But like I said, I just can't help myself.

"Lana, slow down."

The nagging in my ear is real this time. I let my leaden foot off the gas and we instantly slow so that those white lines on the road aren't blurring into one anymore. I didn't even realize I was going so fast.

"Sorry," I say, and turn to offer my grandma a guilty smile.

"Stop thinking about *whatever* you're thinking about and focus on the road."

She folds her arms across herself and wriggles against her seat.

"Are you cold?" Without waiting for an answer, I turn up the heat and turn the fan a level higher.

"It's starting to snow," she says, observing the sparse sprinkle of white flecks flying into our headlights.

"Yep… and we need to stop for gas."

I only now notice our tank is below the one-quarter line. It's another five minutes before I see the next highway exit sign, with a very short list of fast-food locations and gas stations we'll find there. I take the exit. There are two stations on either side of the road, both featuring the same prices. I pull into the righthand parking lot. Easier. Quicker. It looks like we're the only ones here. One other car is parked near the store entrance and likely belongs to the clerk inside. I pull up to Pump #3 and park, kill the engine. My grandma already has her purse in her lap and is digging out her credit card, which she jabs at me like it's a stickup. I take the card without a word.

I pop the gas tank, climb out into the bitter cold. My puffy white coat is plenty warm, but I zip it up all the way anyway, from my chest up to my throat. I insert my grandma's card, rocking on my feet as I wait, until the machine beeps at me to remove the card as if I've forgotten. I start filling up the tank, then lean inside the car to hand back my grandma's card.

"Do you want anything from inside?" I ask. My grandma looks from her credit card to me, then back to her credit card, confused. "My treat," I add.

She shakes her head. "No, use my card."

"You already got gas. Let me buy snacks."

She considers the offer a moment longer before relenting.

"Well, all right. I'd like a Charleston, if they have them."

"I don't think there's a single convenience store in America that doesn't carry Charleston Chews, Grandma."

"Get me a strawberry one."

I nod, grab my black clutch wallet from the center console, and shut the door. The tank is still filling up with gas as I make my way to the convenience store. Its harsh, sterile white lights make me look especially haunting in the front door's reflection. The door dings as I enter. I look to the front counter, where the young and oddly model-esque cashier lifts his square chin to me without expression or enthusiasm. He's got better hair than me, too. My eyes linger on him only for a second before I look at what's behind him—what I've *really* come inside for.

I'm all out of smokes.

I walk casually into the snack aisle, to the candy bars and the bags of hard candies hanging from their pegs. I search out the box of Charleston Chews. The box is pretty much full, flush with the top. I wonder how long these have been sitting on this shelf?

Out of curiosity, I open my wallet to see what I've got. A ten and four singles. My smokes are going to cost me nearly twelve dollars by themselves, I know. Technically I should have enough for my smokes and a single Chew, but…

I stand straight and glance toward the front counter again. The Timothy Chalamet lookalike is on his phone without a care in the world. I unzip my coat again, just a little bit. I stuff my hand into the box of Charleston Chews, into the section with all the strawberry ones my grandma likes so much. I grab as many as my fist can hold and shove them into my coat. My coat's got a neat elastic hem that hugs my hips, ensuring nothing is going to slip out. I zip my coat back up. Then I grab one additional strawberry Chew and take it with me to the front counter. I set it down politely. The cashier looks up from his phone with a bored sigh.

"That everything?"

"Can I also get a pack of American Spirits," I say, pointing to the case at his back. "Blacks."

He opens the case, grabs me a pack, and begins ringing me up without a single thought. I'm mortified. My face burns hot with embarrassment. Shame. Offense.

I'm twenty-six.

I'm only twenty-six!

I'm fairly certain they're supposed to ID anyone under the age of thirty—or rather, anyone whom they believe looks anywhere close to thirty, within reason. It wasn't that long ago I was still getting ID'd to see rated-R movies. There's no way this kid thinks I look older than I am.

Maybe it's all the smoking?

"Aren't you... gonna ask to see my ID?" I loathe the sound of my voice as I say it. Needy.

"Oh, yeah," the kid says, then follows that up with another bored sigh. "Sure."

"Sure..." I mockingly reply, as I'm already fishing my ID from my wallet.

He doesn't even realize I'm doing him a favor—that he'd lose his job like *that* if his boss learned he wasn't checking IDs like he's supposed to. I hand mine over. He takes it, studies it, then studies my face without even a spark of interest or care or anything at all behind those eyes of his. It wasn't five years ago I had boys like him eating out of the palm of my hand. What a twerp, I think. It's not me. It's him. I bet he's probably not even into girls.

"Here you go," he says, and hands me back my ID.

He finishes ringing me up. I hand him all my cash.

"Keep the change," I say, and snatch up my pack of

smokes and my Charleston Chew. I stick the cigarettes into my outer coat pocket on my way to the door.

My heart is thumping and I'm not sure why. It's not like our exchange was heated. And it's not like I'm the least bit nervous about smuggling fifteen bucks' worth of Charleston Chews under my coat. Honestly, I couldn't care less about that.

I hate to admit it, but I think I might be a bit shallow.

I step back into the frigid night. I hurry back to the car, walking briskly but carefully so as not to let the candy slip out of my coat. The gas tank is obviously full by now and the nozzle has shut itself off. I replace it into its holster, shut my gas cap, and then proceed to climb back into the car.

"You're not supposed to leave your car unattended while it's filling up with gas," is the first thing my grandma says to me as I sit heavily behind the wheel and shut my door.

"The car wasn't unattended," I reply. "You were here."

My grandma scoffs, but can't help eyeing me with a certain, humored quirk of her mouth. It's a look that says *'you're lucky I love you so much.'*

I love my grandma, too. Which is why it brings me so much joy to unzip my coat and dump an entire armful of her favorite candy into the cupholders between us.

"Oh my *lord!*" she exclaims. "Lana, I… I didn't say…"

"I know, but we've got a long drive ahead of us."

"One would have done nicely…"

"Now you've got enough to last you the whole week-end, so… you're welcome."

She laughs in disbelief and shoots me another of those questioning glances, like I've lost my mind. She's always looking at me like that. Probably because she's right. I have. Lost my mind, I mean.

I buckle my seatbelt and start the car. My grandma's got her arms folded around herself again, so I turn the heater up yet another level to get us warmed up extra fast.

Before I take us out, I check my phone and see I've got several missed texts, phone calls, and a few voicemails. They're all from *him*. Predictably. I set my phone down without reading or listening to a single one, despite the overwhelming temptation. Let him stew, I think. Let him feel all the things he's made *me* feel. Besides, if I look at anything now I know I'll be tempted to reply, and I think I'm already at my limit for nonsense for the day.

Just like me, however, the night is still so young.

JASPER

$\mathcal{I}$ can't tell if I'm lucky or if the men trying to kill me are just incredibly incompetent, leaving their truck running by the side of the road like they did. I suppose they didn't expect me to have lived through all of that—the gunfire and the wreck. I'm not sure how I survived, either. It might not be for too much longer, though.

My guts hurt.

Like, *really* hurt.

It's like the worst stomach cramp of my life, like somebody's shoved a hot fire poker through my side and left it there, wiggling it around every few seconds for good measure, stirring me up like a hot bowl of soup. My shoulder hurts, too. Same thing. A burning, throbbing sensation. These vague aches and pains are becoming more precise the longer I drive. Pointed. Sharp. I try to focus on the road, but my thoughts keep drifting. The truck keeps drifting, too. I repeatedly jerk the wheel, correcting myself as the truck slides into the road's shoulder. It's hard to tell where the road even ends with all this snow, and it just keeps coming. It's coming down *hard* and *heavy* and it's endless. A proper blizzard.

I eye the bag of money in the passenger seat and wonder if all of this was worth it.

I think maybe I'm dying, actually.

It's getting worse. The pain. It's so powerful, so all-consuming, I can feel it leeching the strength right out of me. As the minutes and miles roll by, I can feel myself relaxing into my seat in a bad way. Like I'm losing control of myself. My hands are colder than ever on the steering wheel, like my circulation is waning, like I don't have enough blood left in me to reach my extremities. Surely it isn't that bad, though, I think. I'm overreacting because I'm scared, is all. I'm scared as hell.

I don't know how much longer I can keep this up.

And that's when I see it. The sign through the snow. It appears faintly at first, so that my eyes notice it but my mind doesn't. I press my foot a little heavier on the gas. The sign's glowing red letters sharpen through the snowfall, until I'm coming up on it, the establishment it advertises, and I hurriedly swap my foot from the gas to the brake. The truck slides, wobbles, fishtails. I let off the brake, try to keep everything under control. I tap the brake instead, but my faculties aren't what they should be.

Because I think maybe I'm dying.

But I'm not entirely sure.

I narrowly avoid sliding the truck into the ditch at the

side of the road as I come to a complete stop. The red sign shines down upon me like some heavenly thing. Or maybe *heavenly* isn't the right word. Red light is hardly ever described as *heavenly*, I suppose. But it's comforting, and to my desperate mind it signals my last chance. I can't drive anymore. I'm already so *tired*, and it's not just the bullets in me, I don't think.

I'm okay. Everything's okay. I just need a break. That's all.

It's all that adrenaline wearing off. I'm crashing now. Naturally. I need to stop for the night before I *really* crash. That would be the smart decision. I need to make the smart decision.

With both hands on the wheel, I gaze up at that sign, its light surely turning my eyes into rubies, and I think to myself what an appropriate name it is for a little refuge like this, out in the middle of nowhere.

The 11th Hour Motel.

I kind of like the sound of that. Just what I need. So I put my foot onto the gas again and, hand over hand, pull into the property. The motel itself is an L-shaped building along the lefthand side of the square lot, and across the back. Standing in the righthand corner of the lot near the road is a separate two-story house that looks like it was plucked straight out of someone's suburb, with an illuminated blue sign in its window that says 'Main Office.' It hurts my eyes to look at that sign, in contrast with the red light glowing upon it.

"Hold on," I tell myself out loud as I steer the truck between the house and motel, where the larger portion of the parking lot sits in back.

There's not a single other car parked back here. Business is *not* booming tonight.

I swing the truck around, pulling up to the row of parking spaces along the house's backside. I wouldn't even know there were parking spaces here if not for the yellow pylons sticking up from the snow to mark them. The truck's headlights shine back at me from the reflection of the house's sliding glass door. I shut them off and kill the engine. The house sits between me and the road. No one passing by could know that I'm here without pulling in themselves.

I unzip the duffel bag on the passenger seat and pause momentarily as I look upon all those bundles of cash. It's a lot. I'm not sure how much. Thanks to my wounds, I'm in no better condition to start estimating now than I was before. Instead I undo one of the bundles and take a few hundreds out, stuffing the bills into my jacket pocket. Then I climb out of the truck.

Hopefully I can pay with cash. I also hope I'm not such a terrible sight that I garner unwanted attention.

The only thing that keeps me from doubling over in pain as I set foot outside the truck is that the act of bending over would only cause me *more* pain. Instead I lean against the truck itself for a moment. Can I hold it together long enough to reserve a room?

What am I even doing here?

I don't trust myself to stay on the road much longer for however many miles are still between me and the next hospital I might visit. I need to check on my wounds. I'll make a better decision then and only then.

Gritting my teeth, I push away from the truck and start

around the house, kicking a few inches of snow with each step. My stomach jostles and aches. I reach the front of the house, step around its corner into the blue light in the window. The light cast on the sidewalk is purple, however, overwhelmed by the giant sign near the road. I hurry to the front door. It's an ordinary door, like I'm about to bother someone at home. Technically I suppose I am. The owners of this motel obviously live here. Will they still be awake, I wonder?

I turn the knob and push my way inside. The door rings an overhead bell, announcing my entrance.

The front room is spacious and has been engineered into something resembling a lobby, with a long counter along the far wall by the foot of the stairs there. The room is dimly lit by a single lamp on said counter. I shuffle forward, shaking fresh snow from my clothes onto the beige carpet. I peer down at my feet, afraid I might be shedding anything else. *Dripping* anything else. So far, so good, although I feel the wet chafe of my jeans against my side, where the denim has obviously soaked up blood.

I lean against the counter, waiting. Did anyone hear the bell over the door? There's another bell on the counter itself, the kind you can tap with a single finger in rapid succession if you want. I'm tempted to do just that, before I notice the sound coming from down the hall. Voices. Music. I shuffle toward the hallway, where I pinpoint the doorway the noise is coming from. It's a movie playing in the other room.

"Hello?"

I return to the little bell and tap it a few times for good measure. I've never been able to use a bell like this without feeling like an asshole somehow. Granted, I have good reason to be in a hurry.

Much to my relief, the noise from down the hall goes quiet. Footsteps approach. From around the corner a woman appears. A *beautiful* woman, I might add. As soon as our eyes lock she adopts a forced smile, one she's learned from years of dealing with the general public. Even so, she's unable to hide her surprise—her eyes wide, eyebrows raised. She probably never expected to receive any guests on a night like this.

"Good evening," she says, and circles around me, around the counter to the other side. Her eyes stay locked onto me the whole way, looking me up and down, from head to toe and back, that disbelieving expression never fading. She's got lovely, sandy hair, which she smooths behind her ear with one hand. "Apologies if you've been waiting. I wasn't expecting to see anyone tonight. I didn't hear the doorbell."

"No, no, you're fine." I swallow and my dry throat makes a loud gulp. "Could you by chance tell me how far to the nearest town? Or…" I pause. "How far to the nearest hospital?"

Her smile falters. A look of concern.

"Is there some kind of emergency?"

"No, no. No emergency. I just…" I force a smile of my own. "I'm traveling quite a ways and might need to stop someplace for some… personal reasons. That's all. Nothing urgent, though."

"I see. Well. The nearest town would be Hodgerton, but it's tiny and there's no hospital there. Your best bet would be the next town west of that, in Morgan. But that's almost an hour drive. On a *good* day. In this weather, I'm not so sure."

I absorb all of this with mounting disappointment. Anxiety. Fear. I can't drive that far in my condition. Although I don't even really know what my condition is. I wonder—if I'm not healthy enough to get myself to a hospital, am I healthy enough to survive the night?

I'm getting ahead of myself. I'm worrying too much. It's not that bad. Not yet. I can make it for one night.

Am I lying to myself?

"All right, that's good to know." I clench my jaw, leaning against the counter as my guts cramp like a ball of constricting snakes inside me. I smile through it, and even manage to fake a bit of a laugh. "I just decided not to test my luck any longer on those roads out there, so... a room for the night would be great."

"I'm glad you didn't," she says, and finally her smile reaches her eyes, which she still refuses to take off me. The manner of her gaze almost startles me, as if maybe she recognizes me. Should I recognize her? Then she seems to remember herself. With a distracted shake of her head, she looks down at her guest logbook on the counter. She spins it around and places a pen on the page, and indicates where she'd like me to fill out my information. "Unfortunately our electronic booking system is down, so I'll need you to sign in here."

I take up the pen. As I begin filling in the first available space with bullshit information, I ask, "Do you accept cash?"

"I do... but I require an additional fifty-dollar deposit for cash payments, which you'll be given back when you check out tomorrow morning. It'll be a hundred-and-fifty for the night total."

A hundred-and-fifty dollars for a seedy little place like this? I suppose if I was paying with a credit card, it would only be an even hundred. Maybe that's not so bad. It's been a while since I last stayed in any motel. Have prices really risen so much?

"That's fine," I say.

I finish signing in. She spins the logbook back toward herself as I reach into my jacket pocket and fish out the hundred-dollar bills. As I remove them, I notice blood on my left hand. The sight of it causes me to flinch. I hope she didn't already notice it. I stuff my hand into my jacket pocket and hand two crisp bills over with the other. She's still reading over the information I wrote down. I don't think she saw. She looks up again and offers me that professional, practiced smile once more, then takes my money, opens up a cash drawer that's hidden on the other side of the counter, and hands me my change, which I immediately stuff into my jacket pocket.

"Do you have a room preference?" she asks.

I have to think for a moment.

"Um... something along the back?"

"Room 19?" she says. "It's the second-to-last room."

"Perfect."

She opens up a wooden cabinet on the wall behind her, where I see the rows of dangling keys inside. She plucks one out and hands it to me. It's a simple key on a keychain, with a flat wooden fob with '19' embossed onto its surface. I take it with my right hand, keeping my left nice and snug and hidden in my jacket.

"I lock up at eleven," she says. "But you're welcome to call anytime with the phone in your room should you need anything."

"All right. Perfect."

"I hope you have a comfortable stay, Peter."

With a kind tilt of her head, her smile broadens, and for the first time I get the sense that it's real, that she's not simply going through the motions of hospitality. I smile back, even if all I really want to do is whimper and moan.

I'm instantly greeted by the bitter cold against my face as I step outside. The wind is screeching overhead. I glance to the big red sign, the snow billowing past, thicker than it was even five minutes ago. It nearly pummels me over as I step around the corner of the house. A strong, continuous, icy gust. I push against it, making my way back to the truck. I grab the bag of money from the passenger seat. It's all I have now. My various wounds all flash with cold fire as I sling the strap onto my shoulder. I lock up the truck and start toward the motel, my room somewhere straight across from the back of the house. The second-to-last room, she said. There's a single lamppost on this side of the parking lot, but its light flickers, sporadically illuminating the visible gusts of snow coming over the roof and over my head.

Room 19. I stick my key into the door, unlock it, and step inside out of the cold. I shut the door behind me. Everything is eerily quiet. The room itself isn't too much warmer than outside. I flip on the light. A queen-sized bed sits on the righthand side of the small room, dressed in an ugly orange and yellow floral pattern comforter. A small dresser sits against the wall on my left. The bathroom is straight across, on the other side of the room. I drop the bag of money onto the bed and make my way there. Each new step is a newer agony.

I flip the bathroom light on—nauseating, headache-inducing, florescent white. I turn to the mirror over the sink and nearly gasp.

"Jesus."

I look like a ghost. I'm pale on an average day, but I'm more than pale now. I'm *gray*. I look clammy. Sweaty. I look like I'm on the brink of unconsciousness, like I can barely hold my eyes open. I reach for the zipper on my jacket. My hands tremble violently. It's a challenge just to grasp the damn thing, pinched between my fingers. I unzip, open it apart, shrug the whole thing off myself and onto the floor at my feet. I actually *do* gasp this time.

Fuck.

There's a lot of blood. So much blood. My shirt is soaked. My pants are soaked. A dizzying wave crashes over me then. I stoop forward and rest my hand against the sink, holding myself up as my legs turn watery. With my other hand, I grasp the hem of my shirt. I have to peel it away from myself, it's stuck to my belly with so much blood.

"Come on…"

I lift my shirt and the sight of the wound sends my legs wobbling. A bullet hole in my side sends a fresh pulse of blood down my abdomen, soaking into the already-soaked waist of my jeans.

"Oh… *oh god…*"

I stumble into the bathroom doorway as a border of *nothingness* constricts my vision.

That's about as far as I make it.

DARLENE

*M*y granddaughter either thinks I'm an idiot or believes herself to be much cleverer than she is. As if I don't already know she has a history. Has she forgotten it was me who picked her up from the station after she shoplifted jewelry at the mall? Granted she'd only been fifteen then. Gosh, has that much time really gone by? Either way, I haven't forgotten, and I haven't failed to notice her other *tendencies* over the years. I know she isn't perfect. I know she's no Shirley Temple. She's her own woman and she's rough around the edges and that's exactly what I love about her.

But for crying out loud, some subtlety would be nice.

I can't help studying the pile of candy in the cupholders between us. I didn't ask for all that. She knows it's unnecessary. She knows it's overboard.

My granddaughter doesn't know when to stop.

I see it in the way she checks her phone each time we come to a red stoplight. I see it in the way she bites her fingernails down to their quicks. I worry about her as much as I love her.

Nevertheless, I take my time nibbling on one of the Charleston Chews she bought for me. Or stole for me. It's cheap gas station candy, so I can't be too upset. I pride myself on knowing how to pick my battles. Better for the two of us to be happy on this journey—we'll be trapped in this car together for another couple days, at least.

I try not to show how nervous I am as the snowstorm gusts against us and Lana's hands barely manage to keep us centered as the road ahead gradually fades away under a perilous layer of snow and ice. We're miles out into nothing now. I can't imagine what we'd do if Lana lost control of the car and we ended up crashed in a snowbank, or worse...

"Slow down a bit," I say, taking another bite of my candy.

"I'm already going slow," Lana says.

"These roads are..." There's a word on the tip of my tongue, but I can't immediately grasp it. It takes me a moment, so that when it finally comes to me I blurt it out far more dramatically than I intend. *"Treacherous..."*

"It's fine," Lana says. However, I see how she grips the wheel even tighter, wringing it in both her hands. "I know how to drive on bad roads."

"Hmm," I say, and nothing more.

Part of me wants to suggest that we turn around and find a motel somewhere, but going back would probably be just as far as whatever the distance is left between us and our next exit.

As if reading my mind, Lana says, "I think we'll stop for the night at the next place we come to. What do you think?"

"I think that sounds marvelous."

I take another bite of my candy. My jaw is already getting sore from all the chewing and the sticking of my teeth. Deciding I've had enough, I look down in search for someplace to store my half-eaten Chew. I decide to simply add it back to the others. As I do, Lana lets out a gasp that launches my heart into my throat.

"Oh my god!"

I look up just in time to see him—a man in the road, arms over his head, squinting through the blowing snow and our oncoming headlights. Lana tries to slow down. The car slides. I feel it. She taps the brakes. I feel that too, as the car tries to slide left and right but can't make up its mind as Lana does her best to control it. The man in the road has since vanished back into the dark flurry of snow in our peripherals, narrowly avoiding being hit. The car judders as Lana brings us to a stop at last, sitting askew in the middle of the road. That's when I see them both. Both men. There are two of them behind our car, caught in the glow of our brake lights, approaching.

"Shit," Lana says.

Without hesitation, she pushes the button on her door that locks each and every other car door. I twist in my seat to see them coming. One of them lags behind the other. I notice his limp. The other man comes to my window as it's closest. I reach for the button to roll it down.

"Don't," Lana says. "We have no idea who these men are."

"Lana, I think they've been in an accident."

"We don't know that."

"Why else would they be walking along the side of the road in this weather?"

The first man stops by my window, hunching down to peer in at us. Still Lana hesitates.

"I'm rolling down my window," I say with finality.

I push the button. The window comes down humming, letting in so much cold in an instant.

"Hi there!" the man calls over the gusting wind. "So sorry about that. I didn't mean to…"

"You nearly got us in an accident," Lana half-shouts at him from across my seat.

"I know, I'm terribly sorry," he says. He doesn't have an especially kind face, I notice. There's a hardness about his eyes, and a look about his mouth, with his mustache and goatee, that somehow gives me the impression that this man doesn't make a habit of smiling. Although I suppose I wouldn't be smiling in his position, either. "We had ourselves an accident of our own, actually."

"Oh dear," I say. I gaze into the surrounding field, but it's all so dark and full of noise, I can't see a thing.

"My buddy here injured his leg in the rollover," the man says, and gestures to his friend who has paused in his approach, lingering instead by the trunk of our car, leaning against it for support.

"Oh dear," I say again.

"Would it be too much trouble if we hitched a ride with y'all into the nearest town? Whichever comes first."

"You guys couldn't call for help or anything?" Lana asks. It's an honest question, but on her tongue it comes out sounding especially pointed. Bothered. Inconvenienced.

"We tried but we've got no service," the man says.

Lana checks her own phone then—for the umpteenth time on our trip—and seems to confirm his claim without another word about it.

"Where are y'all headed?" the man asks.

"Well," I say, taking the reins of this encounter, "to tell you the truth, we're looking to stop at the nearest place we can find."

"That's all right," the man says with a dismissive shake of his head. He's got snow and ice gathering in his hair. "We'll take anything we can get. Just to get out of this storm, if you wouldn't mind."

"Hold on just a second," Lana says, and suddenly my window is rolling back up, rolling shut right in the poor man's face.

"Lana!" I say. The window closes. The man outside straightens where he stands, but doesn't move. "What on earth are you doing?"

"It's not the 1950s anymore, Grandma. You don't just let strange men into your car. Especially not when you're... you know, *us.*"

"Oh my goodness, you can't possibly think they're out here preying on people in a storm like this! That's just... *crazy.* You're being crazy..."

"It's not crazy, Grandma."

"They wrecked their car, for crying out loud. This would either have to be the most elaborate setup for an ambush I ever heard of, or they'd have to be *very* opportunistic men to even consider what you're thinking at a time like this."

"Maybe they wrecked their car. I don't know. Do you see a wrecked car anywhere?"

I can't help but scoff at my granddaughter's ridiculousness.

"When's the last time we even saw another vehicle on this road tonight?" I say. "If their plan was to hurt somebody, they could have picked a more worthwhile time and place…"

After another brief moment of thought, Lana relents. She rolls my window back down. The man outside stoops again to see us. This time I see the snowflakes snagged in his mean, bushy eyebrows.

"You're welcome to ride with us to the nearest stop," Lana tells him.

"Thank you," he says. He smiles then, but it's merely the faintest hint of a smile. It's so cold outside, I can't say I really blame him for a stiff face. "Thank you so much."

Lana unlocks the back doors. The man gestures for his buddy to climb in on the other side. They each climb into the car with their bags—a traveling case and something else with a strap—and take their seats with much groaning and panting. I can vicariously feel the relief in each of them as they shut their doors on the cold outside, sitting in the warmth of our car's circulating heat.

"Thank you so much for the ride," the other man says. I crane my neck to see him over my shoulder, sitting behind Lana's seat. This man has a much kinder face than the other. Pudgier, too. He looks at me directly as I turn to see him, and nods with a deeply grateful grin on his face. "Thank you, ma'am. And miss." He glances to the rearview mirror, where Lana is watching them both with sharpened eyes.

"What are your names?" I ask.

The kinder-faced man looks momentarily surprised by the question.

"Carl. You can call me Carl. And my friend here—"

"Jason," the other man says. I twist a little more to see him behind my seat. His eyes don't even meet mine, however. He remains focused on Lana, or rather on the back of her head.

"It's nice to meet you both," I say. I turn back around in my own seat. "I'm sorry to hear about your trouble. These roads are positively *treacherous* tonight."

"That they are," Jason says. "That they are…"

"Thank you again," Carl says. "It means a lot, you stopping like you did…"

"Didn't have much of a choice…" Lana mutters under her breath. Luckily, I'm not sure the men in the back could hear her remark over the sound of the blowing heater.

"Yes, we appreciate your generosity," the man called Jason says. "And I completely understand your hesitation."

"Oh, one-hundred percent," Carl says. "You never know who you can trust these days."

"Isn't that the truth," Lana mutters again.

I want to smack her arm, but I resist. Again, I don't think the men can hear her as well as I can. Instead I twist back around in my seat.

"It's no trouble at all," I tell them. "We're happy to help."

Lana begins to drive again—or tries to. Our tires spin on the icy road for a bit, the car sliding further out of place, before finally we seem to find purchase on the asphalt and lurch forward, moving slowly. I sigh a breath of relief. All in all, I'm actually quite proud of my granddaughter. Not just for being uncharacteristically cautious, but also for her ability to handle the car in such circumstances.

Everyone falls silent as we start to move again. Too silent for my liking, with strangers sitting behind me. I eye all that candy still sitting in the cupholder between Lana and myself. I grab a couple of them, and turn in my seat to face the shivering men behind me.

"Charleston Chew?"

MISSY

I'm halfway through my movie when I hear a voice in the hallway, shortly followed by a series of dings from the bell on the counter. I can hardly believe it. A guest? Tonight? I pause my movie, jump out of my seat, and straighten my sweater vest as I hurry into the hall.

The man I find standing in the lobby startles me.

He looks like a ghost.

He seems friendly enough as I greet him, however, if not a bit distracted. That's perfectly all right, considering I'm feeling quite distracted myself. He asks me a series of strange questions—he's looking for the nearest hospital? What could that possibly be about?—but mostly my mind is circling something else entirely.

He looks like a ghost.

For starters, there's the color of his skin. He's paler than the snow outside. A sickly kind of pale. A bloodless kind of pale. I try my best not to appear concerned or bewildered by his appearance, which requires me to muster the phoniest smile I can. There's something clearly wrong with this man, something I believe he's trying to conceal. But there's also something else about him. Something that disorients me.

He looks like a ghost… in more ways than one.

Beyond the frightful state of his appearance, this man is uncannily familiar to me. I know his face. I have seen his face before, although I am quite certain I have never met this particular man in my life. It's not entirely unlike the feeling I get watching my favorite movie, when I gaze upon the lead actor's handsome visage.

He looks like *you*.

I go through the motions of checking him into a room. I catch myself staring, studying him too closely, and I see it in his eyes that he notices. But I don't stop. While he signs into the logbook, I can't help but trace the features of his face with my eyes, features which so closely resemble yours that I can hardly believe it.

Eventually I hand him his key and watch as he makes his way outside. The cool burst of air that comes through the doorway as he goes touches me clear across the room behind the counter, caressing my face like a deathly hand upon my cheek. A chill races up my neck and scalp and I shiver.

Did you have a brother I never knew about? That is how close the resemblance is, I swear it. You would agree with me, I know it. If you were still here, I could stand the two of you together, face to face, and you'd think you were looking into a mirror! Albeit a time-altering mirror, I suppose, as this man looks like a younger version of you—the versions of us I remember best.

Shortly after the door is closed, I scamper around the desk and practically race down the hall and into the kitchen at its end. I leave the light off as I pull the curtain aside from the sliding glass door and peer into the dark parking lot out back. His vehicle, a truck, is parked *right* there, and I nearly gasp as I see him there so close. He reaches into the passenger side to grab something. I pull back a little, letting the curtain fall so that just a sliver of the window is uncovered, my face surely hovering there behind the glass like a spying ghoul. He makes his way from his truck to his room. There's something wrong about his gait, I notice. He shuffles like an old man when he's clearly anything but. I think he might be ill, but in what way I'm not sure.

He disappears into his room. The light comes on in Room 19's window. With a heavy sigh, I let the curtain fall back into place. I stand in the dark of our kitchen for a time, thinking about him, thinking about you. Then I return into the living room where my movie is still paused, and I realize I paused it once again with the lead actor frozen on screen. He looks *less* like you now than I previously thought. I think it's because of that man. The guest in Room 19 looks so much more like you, that suddenly I realize this Hollywood version doesn't do you justice at all.

A part of me longs to see him again. To study him if only for a moment.

My heart hurts in the best way.

Leaving my movie paused, I proceed back down the hall, through the lobby and to the stairs, my feet dancing upon each step. I cross the wide upstairs hallway to our bedroom on the left. I leave the light off as I cross immediately to our dresser, to the drawer where I keep your softest sweaters. I remove one of them. A thick, green, wool sweater. I take it to the foot of our bed, where I sit and bury my face into it, breathe it in. It hardly smells of you anymore. Mostly it smells old. Of dust.

Not much in this house smells like you these days. It's been too long.

I set the sweater aside disappointedly. The ache in my heart is too powerful to ignore. It's a painfully beautiful feeling. I know my movie downstairs will help—it usually does—but somehow it doesn't seem like enough in this moment. Suddenly I wish to burst into tears. That alone would let off this steam inside me. But somehow I can't mange that, either. My eyes remain stubbornly dry. My movie will help to lubricate the floodgates, at the very least…

I return downstairs, reluctantly dragging my feet, and halt at what I see on the floor near the front counter.

Red droplets on our beige carpet.

I drop to my knees to inspect. I gently touch my finger to the stained fibers—to the spots of blood that are still damp.

"Oh, God," I murmur, as I observe the crimson residue that comes away on the pad of my index finger.

My guest isn't just ill. He's hurt. Bleeding. *Badly.*

I return to my feet and freeze.

Suddenly his asking about the nearest hospital makes complete sense. What a fool he must be to take his chances *here,* when he obviously needs emergency medical attention. If he's bleeding enough to drip on my carpet, there's no telling just how urgent his injuries might be. I recall the manner in which he concealed his hand in his pocket. Could it be that his hand is injured? I suppose it's possible his wound isn't fatal. But the utter *state of him*, the color of him, the manner in which he carried himself across the parking lot to his motel room door—no, this is more than any mere hand injury.

I can't lie, I'm irritated that he's bled on our carpet. I'm going to have to scrub it out as soon as possible. And the idea that he's now in one of our rooms bloodying up the carpet there, as well as the bedsheets and whatever else, makes me *seethe*.

Why on *earth* is he here?

Moving with haste, I grab my ring of motel keys from the counter, pull on my boots, lace them up, grab my coat from the coatrack by the door, stuff myself into it, and zip it up with one violent tug. Then I pull the hood over my head as I walk out the door, kicking through the snow.

You careless, thoughtless fool.

I lower my face to avoid the blast of cold wind that comes as I turn the corner and begin making my way toward the back half of the motel. So much snow has already covered everything. The parking lot is one solid sheet of white, glittering under the flickering lamppost. I keep forgetting to fix that.

I stomp my boots on the mat outside Room 19 and rap my knuckles on the door five times. I wait. There's no answer. I knock again. I wait. Same thing.

Like hell I'm letting you die in my motel.

I pull out my ring of keys and cycle through each one until I have 19's in my hand. I unlock the door with ease. I push my way in, sweeping my gaze across the dimly lit room until I see him, slumped in the bathroom doorway with his hands full of blood, his eyes rolled up into the back of his skull.

QUENTIN

*T*he old woman is chatty as hell. Chattier than I can stand. She introduces herself as Darlene, and introduces her granddaughter as Lana. At the sound of her name leaving her grandmother's lips, Lana shifts and squirms in her seat. She's a beautiful girl, I can't help thinking to myself. Even for a total bitch. I've met plenty of women like her in my time on this earth—young, beautiful, and *mean.* They mistake their meanness for strength, a show of power. It's a form of compensation, no different than the false machismo you see displayed by men compensating for their own... *shortcomings,* so to speak.

"It's lovely to meet you, Darlene," Allen says beside me, laying it on extra thick. It's also possible he's being sincere. It's hard to tell with him sometimes.

"It's also lovely to meet you, Lana," I add, and watch from behind as she grimaces, which delights me, I can't lie.

She says nothing in reply, but her grandmother proceeds to flood the car with her friendly chatter. I tune her out for the most part. Allen seems perfectly content handling the back and forth. What a lonely man he must be, I think.

I spend the next several slogging miles peering out my window into the blizzard, then glancing back to the young woman behind the wheel. Every now and again I glance into the rearview mirror where our gazes occasionally meet. She's truly a sight for sore eyes, I must say. At least there's *that*. Even if she's clearly brimming with disdain when she catches me watching her, as if my gaze alone is an affront.

She's beautiful in the same way a diamondback is beautiful—wild, probably unstable, never to be trusted.

"So, where are you two coming from?" the old woman asks.

I intend to let Allen answer, but the dumb bastard's tongue seems mute suddenly.

"We've come all the way from Ohio," I lie. "A long, *long* roadtrip to see some family."

"Oh!" Darlene exclaims. "Are you brothers?"

"That's right," I lie again. "Brothers."

"I thought you were friends?"

I glance to the rearview mirror and catch Lana watching me with slitted eyes.

"Earlier you called Carl your buddy…"

I feel myself bristling. I have to force my voice to remain unbothered.

"Did I say that?"

"Yeah, you said *'my buddy here hurt his leg'* or something like that."

I force a laugh. "Ah, right. Is that weird? To call your brother your buddy?"

"Of course it's not," Darlene speaks up. She gently slaps

her granddaughter's arm beside her. "I apologize for my granddaughter. She likes to nitpick things. It's nothing personal, I can assure you..."

"Oh, no offense taken," I say.

"This is why she has no luck with men. None whatsoever..."

"Oh my *God*..." Lana groans. She glances at her grandmother only for a moment, the horror on her face nearly causing me to burst into a giggling fit. She focuses on the road again, her scowl plain as day along the contours of her face.

"Well, it's the truth," Darlene says. She shifts in her seat as she turns around to face us. "You would never believe it looking at her, of course. She's got a broken *picker,* is the problem. The absolute *worst* taste in men, hands down..."

"Jesus, Grandma, *stop...*"

"Well, Darlene," I say, "it's nothing to do with the genes that obviously run in your family, I can tell you that."

Darlene's eyes light up as she turns around in her seat again, so that she can properly throw her head back and laugh. I meet Lana's gaze in the rearview mirror once more. She's fuming now.

"If your smile is even half as lovely as your grandmother's, Lana, I'm sure you'll be just fine. You've just gotta remember to show it once in a—"

My words are interrupted as the car gives a sudden jerk, throwing me against the back of Darlene's seat. We're sliding. Lana carefully navigates us, tapping the brakes until suddenly we straighten out almost as violently as we started sliding in the first place. I adjust myself back into my seat, my heart thump, thump, thumping in my chest. In an instant everyone's gone deathly silent.

"Sorry about that, everyone," Lana announces with as much phony exasperation as she can summon. "I lost control for a second. Jason, are you not wearing your seatbelt?"

Darlene cranes her neck to see me, confirming for herself that I am not, in fact, wearing my seatbelt.

"Jason, put on your seatbelt, for God's sake!" she says.

I exchange another glance with Lana in the rearview— her gaze heated enough to defrost the windshield all on its own, if she allowed it. Obviously she'd performed her little accident on purpose. I buckle my seatbelt to put an end to the drama before it starts.

"There," I say. "My mistake."

I know Lana and I have one thing in common, at least.

Neither of us can wait until this damned ride is over.

JASPER

One moment I'm losing my ability to stand, my strength bleeding out of me like warm piss down my leg—or like the literal blood down my abdomen—and the next I'm waking up, blinking sleep from my eyes in some strange room I don't recognize.

It's not my motel room. Someplace else. I'm lying in a warm bed, the light turned low. This room is cluttered with personal effects. An overfull bookshelf, a dresser lined with framed photographs, a desk in the corner littered with ribbons and pieces of cloth draped about an old sewing machine.

I'm naked under the covers.

I snap upright and immediately wince at the pain across my middle, across my back. Gingerly, I lift the covers off myself. There's a wide cotton gauze wrapped several times over around my stomach. I don't remember anything after losing consciousness, but it appears I've been medically tended to. My mind races to piece together what I *do* remember—driving on those icy roads, pulling into the motel parking lot, barely managing to check into my room without giving away my grave condition. Apparently I failed on that front.

Is that where I am, then? Back in that woman's house? The owner? I wonder how she was able to haul me back to her—

I startle as the bedroom door cracks open. She appears there, peeking in politely. When she sees that I'm awake, that I'm sitting up a bit, she smiles warmly and enters the room. Her hands are full, carrying a bedside tray with a steaming hot bowl of what I presume to be vegetable soup, by the aroma. My stomach growls at just the sight of the steam.

She comes to stand next to me. She's got an apron tied around her waist and her sandy blonde hair is pulled over one shoulder. She sets the tray of food on the nightstand there, then turns to me with her hands clasped against her belly, her head tilted in a kind sort of way.

"How are you feeling?"

I'm not sure what to say. I'm feeling much better, in terms of the excruciating pain I was fighting against before. I lift the covers on myself once more to study the bandages around my stomach. I'm not *totally* naked under the covers, either. I'm wearing boxer shorts, though they're not mine.

"I hope you'll forgive me," she said. "Your clothes were soaked in blood. I thought it best to change you after I finished patching you up."

"You patched me up?"

"Well, yes," she says. "You were in a bad state, Peter…" She pauses, straightens her tilted head as her eyes narrow upon me. "…or should I call you Jasper?"

Before I can answer or even begin to think up an excuse, a *lie,* she continues.

"Either way, you must be in some terrible trouble. Judging by your wounds, and that big ol' bag of money I found on your bed, I think I can safely guess the *kind* of trouble you're in."

"You haven't called anyone, have you?" I blurt out. "The police, I mean. I can't have the police involved…"

She rests those narrowed eyes on me for a while longer, not saying a word, although the corners of her mouth carry the hint of a smile. Her clasped hands separate, finding their way onto either of her hips.

"Don't worry yourself. I haven't called anyone." She smooths her apron and takes a seat on the edge of the bed beside me. She places a single hand upon the shape of my leg under the covers. "You're lucky you ended up here of all places, you know. I can't imagine many other motel owners around these parts have extensive backgrounds as field medics like I do."

"A… a field medic?"

"Yes. I was in the military." She sighs wearily. "I've done the best I can, all things considered. I've stopped your bleeding and disinfected what I could, but you'll still need additional treatment I can't provide. I've only bought you time. The bullet passed through your midsection, but there's no telling what kind of havoc it wreaked in between. You'll need to sit tight for the remainder of the night."

"But I'll live?" The words come out sounding so much more fretful than I mean them to, betraying my anxiety.

"You'll live. And if the storm has cleared up enough by

morning, we'll see about getting you to the nearest hospital."

I'm starting to hurt again, sitting up like I am, so I collapse back onto my pillow, lying flat, and utter the sorriest *thank you* I can manage. I breathe through my teeth, as the pain in my stomach ebbs and flows.

"You'll still experience some pain, of course," she says. "If it's too much, I can offer you some more painkillers. Do you think you can eat something?"

She stands from the bed and moves to the tray of food on the nightstand. The vegetable soup. It smells delicious. I *am* hungry, I think, but my hunger is lost somewhere in the confusion of pain and worry, so it's hard to get an actual read on myself.

"You should eat," she adds.

After already lying down again, it feels impossible to sit back up. I try anyway. She immediately moves to help me, and positions my pillow behind my head so it's not such a strain.

"There. That comfortable?"

"Yes. Thank you…"

She takes a seat on the edge of the bed again, this time *right* beside me, hovering. Her eyes are kinder at this distance, I notice. Warm and deep. And that hint of a smile is clearer on her lips. She takes the hot bowl of soup into her hands. The steam wafts up between us, obscuring her face, and a strange sensation comes over me then, one I can't readily explain or rid myself of—the sudden, inexplicable sense that none of this is real. Like I'm dreaming. As if I could wake at any moment. It's accompanied by a wave of wooziness. Nausea. Maybe it's that I've lost so much blood.

Or maybe the steam and warm soup aroma have triggered my hunger even more, and I've become lightheaded with it. Disoriented. Either way, as her face becomes veiled in white steam, my mind feels as though it's slipping again, like it did before when I fainted in the motel room. The shadows threaten to swallow my vision. I hold on. I *try* to hold on.

"Stay with me," she says.

I take a deep breath. I listen to the clink of her silver spoon inside the bowl, and suddenly she's touching the hot spoon to my lips. I open my mouth and she tips it in. It tastes incredible. The soup washes over my tongue and down my throat and I feel my entire body warm with it. Another spoonful. I swallow it greedily. Unfortunately, the surrounding darkness still appears to be greedily swallowing me as well.

"It's going to be all right," she says.

I feel myself *melting*. My body losing its shape. Spilling into the bed.

Another spoonful. I barely possess the faculties to swallow this time. I'm so limp and *relaxed* I can hardly understand how my mind is still hanging on. By a single thread, it seems.

"Everything's going to be all right, Geoffrey..."

On the brink of fading into nothing, my mind catches on her words—snags on one in particular.

Jasper, I want to say but can't. My tongue is much too heavy in my mouth. *My name is Jasper.*

And then the darkness finally takes me.

LANA

*T*he roads are steadily getting worse and my confidence in keeping us in our lane is waning. I feel the tires slipping and losing traction every half mile or so. What's worse, is I can feel the others' eyes on me the whole way. They don't trust my abilities. But ability will only get you so far, anyway, on roads like these, on tires like ours. I believe I'm doing the best anyone could.

I feel Jason's eyes on me most of all. The prick. For being a complete stranger, he sure makes a damn strong first impression, and it's not a good one. I'd like to leave him stranded on the side of the road again, except I know my grandma would take his side. I can't believe her, either. There's no doubt in my mind we're going to fight about this later. Mostly because I'm planning for it. I'm not letting it go. To say those things about me, to two strange men we just picked up off the side of the road—is she insane? I think she might be. Either way, I feel betrayed.

These thoughts are still eating at me when I lose control of the car. Complete control. The wheel jerks in my hands and we start to slide. My grandma gasps. The men in back say nothing at all. Not only do we slide, we *spin,* until suddenly we're facing the other way, sliding backwards. I've taken my foot completely off the gas, my hands gripping the useless wheel. We continue to spin until we've come full circle, still sliding, still sliding, until the car stops with a violent *whump* against the snow bank along the side of the road.

For a moment, everything is silent and still.

I crank the wheel away from the snow bank and apply gas, but nothing happens. I put the car into REVERSE and ease my foot onto the gas but we don't move an inch.

"Goddammit."

"Lana!" my grandma says, as if I haven't heard her say so much worse.

"What? We're stuck."

My grandma leans forward in her seat, peering across the hood of our car where the headlights glare against the snow they're resting against.

"You're going to have to get out and push," she says. She looks at me, then peers into the backseat. "You, too, Jason. Carl can't, of course, with his leg…"

"Give it some gas," Jason tells me, as if I haven't already tried that. Anything to avoid having to get off his lazy ass, I suspect.

"I already tried. We're stuck."

"You two get out and let me behind the wheel," my grandma says. "I'll give it gas while you push. Come on, now. Let's get this over with."

I want to groan but I resist. I step out of the car, into the ice and snow and gravel. My seventy-two-year-old grandma shimmies her way out of her seat and into mine, behind the wheel. She rolls down the window.

"Holler when you're ready," she says. "I'll apply the gas nice and slow."

She's done this before, of course.

Surprisingly, Jason climbs out as well. I expected more resistance from him. I suppose he realizes he has no choice if he ever wants to be rid of us.

We each make our way to the front of the car. Luckily I'm wearing my boots. I step into the snow ahead of the headlights, where I've just enough room to crouch down and place my hands against the front bumper. Jason hesitates along the side of the hood, studying me, studying the snowbank he's going to have to step into if he actually means to help.

"Thank God we picked you guys up," I say. "Or I'd be pushing this all by myself."

His eyes dart toward me only for a second, but even in such a brief glance I see he's bubbling with contempt for me. *Good.* Let his hatred fuel him as we push the car back onto the road.

I brace with my hands against the freezing bumper. Jason finally comes to stand next to me, where he crouches down and presses against the car the same as I do.

"Ready!" I scream, just as a gust of icy wind howls against me.

I'm not sure if my grandma heard me or not. I open my mouth to scream again when suddenly I hear the tires beginning to spin, little by little, my grandma giving the gas gentle taps.

"Push," I growl, and follow my own advice.

Jason pushes as hard as I do, each of us straining our bodies against the headlights. I don't feel the car moving even an inch. I heave myself against the car in repeated bursts, as if I can rock it into motion. I think it might actually be working. Or maybe Jason is simply pushing much harder than I am and making up for my soft, spindly body. I feel my boots crushing the snow down into ice, as they begin to slip out from under me. I barely keep standing. Then suddenly the car actually *moves,* reversing backward out from under our pushing hands. Jason goes down onto his knees before sprawling flat onto the ice without the car there to hold him upright. It takes all my effort not to laugh. Even so, I instinctively move toward him, offering a hand to help him up. He pushes himself up onto his hands and knees. He swipes the air between us, dismissing my outstretched hand.

Well, fuck you, too, I think.

As he hunches there for a moment, getting his feet under himself, I catch sight of something down the front of his jacket, glimmering in the light of the glaring head-lights before us—something oil-black and snug against his side.

I'm pretty sure it's a gun.

Then he's up and standing again, wiping snow from his front.

"Thanks for the help," I say. I mostly mean it, though I'm frowning as I say it. I can't help it.

Jason doesn't even look at me as he starts back to the car, where my grandma's parked and climbed back into her seat already. Pretty spry for a seventy-two-year-old woman, I have to admit. I get behind the wheel again.

"Not too shabby," my grandma tells us. "That could have been a lot worse."

I put the car into DRIVE again. Before I press on the gas, however, I glance into the rearview, at Jason in the backseat. He's still paying me no mind. But all I can think about is the gun strapped under his arm beneath his jacket. I suppose it's not the most uncommon thing. Lots of people carry concealed firearms.

Either way, my annoyance is suddenly replaced with something else—a feeling I'd rather not have while giving two complete strangers a lift in my car.

"A lot worse," I say, repeating my grandma's words.

Then we resume our journey like nothing ever happened.

MISSY

*H*e reminds me of you that much more with his eyes closed. Serene. Angelically handsome. Not only that, but his breaths whistle through his nostrils while he sleeps, like yours used to. Is that not the most curious thing? I'm not joking anymore—did you have a younger brother I never knew about? He could be your twin.

Once he's asleep, I place the bowl of soup back onto the tray on the nightstand. Then I sit for a few minutes and just watch him. It hurts to see him, but in a good way. A pleasant ache in my chest. It's difficult to pry my eyes away.

Finally I take my leave, closing the guest bedroom door behind myself. I begin untying my apron as I descend the stairs into the lobby. I continue past the front desk, where his blood still stains the carpet underneath. I think there might be some blood on the stairs as well, after dragging him up there like I had to. I'm only one woman, after all.

I take my apron into the kitchen where I hang it beside

the fridge. Then I turn to our little dining table, where I've laid out all his things—his bag of money, his wallet, his phone, the keys to his truck. His *gun.* I hate guns. Truly. Just the sight of it makes me queasy, even a little one like this. I hesitate to even keep it. Deciding I want nothing to do with the pistol, I take it and toss it into the trash, where I've already stuffed Jasper's bloody clothes. Out of sight, out of mind.

Returning to the table, I pull the bag open once again and gaze upon all the bundles of cash inside. The sight of *that* gives me butterflies. I've never cared much about money, but I can't help marveling all the same. Money's too important to ignore, whether we like it or not.

Where did this money come from? What did he do to get it? Who might be searching for it? Obviously whoever put those bullets in him. More butterflies inside me. I should have asked him about that. Truthfully, however, I don't want to know. The more I know, the more danger I'm in. But it would be reassuring to know he already took care of his hunters, that he didn't merely *survive* them. Oh well, it's too late to ask now.

I grab his wallet and take another gander inside. It's empty, as far as money goes. I've already looked at his ID, where I learned his real name. Jasper is a much more handsome name than Peter, I think.

Jasper.

He even resembles you in his photo ID. The same sweet, innocent eyes. A boyishness that'll last him well into his later years, undoubtedly. I didn't think it possible that I could miss you more than I already do, but this man has torn old wounds open afresh and I can scarcely patch mine like I can his.

I stuff his wallet into my pant pocket, along with his keys. Next I pick up his smartphone. I tap the screen and am promptly asked for a fingerprint to bypass.

Easy enough.

I return upstairs. I open the guest bedroom door and poke my head inside. The lamp on the nightstand casts a cozy warm glow over the room. From the door, I can tell he hasn't moved an inch since I left him. He's sleeping like the dead. I take a seat on the edge of the bed beside him like before.

"Jasper? Are you awake?"

Of course he's not. I set his phone in my lap and hold his limp hand between both of mine, feeling the warmth of his palm. He might be sleeping like the dead, but he's as warm as an oven. You were that way, too, I remember. So incredibly warm. A human furnace. Once again I'm reminded of what I've been missing all these years, these lonesome winters colder than I can stand.

I place his warm hand over my breast. I cup it there, only for a moment. A few seconds. That's how long it takes before I realize what I'm doing, before I remember myself and shudder with shame.

I wake his phone once more, presenting me with its lockscreen. I press his thumb to the fingerprint reader. The phone vibrates softly as the screen unlocks. It worked. I sigh with relief and give him back his hand, folded across his belly.

He's received new text messages within the last couple hours from a woman named 'Jennifer.' I open the conversation. The latest message received reads: *Are you good? Text me ASAP.*

I scroll through many texts between them and quickly notice the terms of endearment sprinkled throughout. *Babe. Baby. Sexy.* I scroll farther than I should, delving deep into a past that's none of my business but I can't resist.

An image stops me dead in my tracks.

My heart gongs in my chest. In my throat. I nearly recoil, but my eyes are glued. Transfixed. My stomach twists into knots. I'm breathing hard through my open mouth. My tongue's gone dry.

I'm confronted with the image of a nude woman. She's splayed herself apart on the floor before a bedroom mirror, her dark hair pulled over one bare shoulder, her lopsided mouth lifting one side with a devious smirk. When finally I can tear my gaze away from the lewd photograph, my eyes dart to him instead, lying in our guest bed none the wiser. His sleeping face still reminds me of you, but now I notice something else there… something more painful than any mere resemblance.

What kind of man wants anything to do with trash like this?

I see that in him now. It's not just a boyishness. The boyishness is part of the illusion. It's an effortless, dangerous charm. A weaponized charm. This is a man who is wholly aware of his good looks and will not hesitate to use them for his own gain, however impure, however debased they might be.

I daringly look to the photo again. She's just the same. They're a match. I can see that now. My heart still hasn't stopped angrily pounding. I'm tense through my every limb, on the brink of trembling as I hold his phone in my hands, yet I proceed to scroll farther still. Only a little more. A little more is all it takes before I'm confronted by another shock. It's a shock I should have expected. And perhaps I did expect it.

I lower the phone as quickly as I see it. Then I steal another glance. Only briefly. I look to the man beside me. He is not at all the man I assumed he might be. To exchange photographs like these... I can hardly understand it. The impulsiveness. The recklessness. The shamelessness. I'd be lying if I said I hadn't already seen him naked, but that was innocent. That was necessary. He'd needed a change of clothes, as his were covered in blood, and I'd also needed to check him for additional wounds. But *this*. The flesh I've seen displayed on his phone's screen was not intended for me, but it shouldn't have been intended for *anyone*, is my thinking.

Why is my heart still beating so fast?

Why is my tongue still so deathly dry?

Why am I burning up inside with these... *unforgivable* sensations?

I take a third glance at the image on the screen and those sensations flare hot and piercing. Annoyance. Disgust. Jealousy. *Arousal.*

I swallow and my throat makes a wet, noisy gulp.

I power the whole thing off. That's enough snooping for one day. For a lifetime. I shouldn't have done that. Why did I do that? I'm better than this.

Control yourself.

I stand up from his bed. I let my gaze linger on him, on his softly lit face, the Cupid's bow of his lips glistening with sweat. He swallows in his sleep and his throat makes a sound like mine just did, his Adam's apple bobbing sharply underneath.

Control yourself.

I turn and flee into the hall. That's what I do. I *flee.* From my own emotions and impulses which I apparently can't trust at the moment. I flee into my bedroom, to my night-stand, where I open the bottom drawer and toss his phone inside. I fish his wallet from my pocket and toss it into the drawer as well, followed by the keys to his truck. Then I slam the drawer shut and put it all out of my mind.

LANA

*I*t sneaks up on me like a mirage. I'm not sure if what I'm seeing is real at first, like my eyes are playing tricks, or something in the car has spontaneously decided to reflect on the windshield, creating the illusion of light in the distance. But not just light.

Red light.

It glows through the slanting white of the blizzard like an ember in the dark, growing brighter, stronger. My grandma shifts in her seat as she presumably notices it as well.

"Do you see that?" she says, leaning forward.

"I see it."

Less distance makes the light grow sharper, clearer, until the light tightens into shapes, into *words*. It's an actual sign, lit up like something along the Las Vegas Strip.

The 11th Hour Motel, it reads.

We're already moving at a snail's pace, but I allow the car to slow even more as we approach. The house beneath the sign reveals itself similarly, the first-floor window alight with a sign of its own that reads: *Main Office*. We come to a complete stop. The big sign looms over us, dousing us in its red glow. Farther in the distance, the road ahead fades into the black-and-white static of the storm. I see no other lights that way. If there's a town nearby, this little establishment seems to be on the outskirts.

"What do you think?" I ask my grandma. "Do we stop here, or do we keep—"

"We stop here," my grandma interrupts. Then, into the backseat she says, "I hope you're both all right if we stop for the night. I don't dare push our luck any longer on these roads."

Both men nod their approval.

Easing my foot back onto the gas, I crank the wheel and turn us into the property's entrance. The motel itself is a dingy little thing on our lefthand side and across the back of the property, as my shining headlights soon reveal. I drive us slowly past the "Main Office", to the parking lot at its rear. I pull straight ahead, into what I assume is the parking space for Room 16 along the back. The gold-plated 16 on the door gleams prettily in the headlights. I already plan to request the key to that room specifically, for my grandma's sake. The less walking across the icy parking lot, the better.

Sixteen, sixteen, sixteen, I repeat in my mind to remember.

I park the car. Then I glance into the rearview mirror and notice something that makes my blood run cold.

Jason is reaching into his jacket—reaching for the holstered gun I saw there before.

"Hey, you see this?" Carl says, and smacks Jason's arm to get his attention.

Jason pauses. He glances first to the mirror—to me—where we briefly make eye contact, before quickly following Carl's gaze toward the back of the house behind us. Carl indicates something there—a large pickup truck parked against the back of the house.

"You know that truck?" I ask, watching closely as Jason removes his hand from his jacket. Empty.

"I think…" He falters, staring over his shoulder through the rear windshield. "I think that might be our buddy's truck, yeah."

"Oh!" my grandma says excitedly. "What good luck! I bet his truck handles much better in the snow than our little car, too."

"It *might* be his truck," Jason emphasizes as he turns around in his seat. He smiles at the both of us up front. "Maybe. We'll see."

Thank God, I think to myself. I pray that it is their friend's truck and we never have to interact with them again. The thought of meeting them again in the morning to drive them farther into town already occurred to me. I think I'd rather be shot in the back of the head by Jason's concealed firearm than give him another ride.

"Do you two have enough money for a room tonight?" my grandma asks. Always so considerate.

"We should," Carl assures us. "But thank you for asking."

I'd almost think Carl genuinely sweet, if not for the company he chooses to keep.

My grandma retrieves her credit card from her purse and hands it to me.

"For the room," she says.

I don't argue. I have no money and I can't exactly shoplift a motel room.

"I'll be right back."

I leave the car running as I step out into the swirling cold. Jason steps out of the car as well and hastily makes his way across the lot, toward the *Main Office.* I pull my coat's hood over my head, fold my arms across myself, and hurry along behind him. The blustering snow flecks noisily against the back of my hood. Ahead of me, Jason vanishes around the corner of the house. By the time I reach it, hurrying along the front walkway, I see him step inside, letting the door fall shut behind him.

Asshole.

I push the door open just a moment behind, the bell over the door announcing us. The house's warmth envelops me in an instant like a warm hug. Jason stands near the front counter, beside what appears to be a wash bucket on the floor. It looks like someone made a mess. There's a wet patch of carpet that's just been recently scrubbed.

Jason begins aggressively tapping the bell on the counter. *Ding ding ding ding ding ding.* Wherever the owner is, I'm immediately annoyed on their behalf. Then Jason leans against the counter with one elbow, and side-eyes me with bald-faced loathing.

Right back at you, I say with my eyes in kind.

He directs his gaze elsewhere. Above us, there comes the sound of a door closing shut, followed by footsteps toward the head of the stairs. I gaze that way as she appears

—a woman with gorgeously long, sandy hair falling about her shoulders. She looks surprised to see us, her eyes wide and bulging. She wipes her mouth on the back of her hand as if she were just in the middle of eating dinner—or perhaps brushing her teeth.

It's only as she begins descending the stairs with particularly careful foot placements that I notice the other wet patches of scrubbed carpet along the stairway's length.

Before she can say a word to us—before I can say a word to her—Jason steps forward and announces his intentions.

"I'd like to book a room for the night," he says, as though we'd be here for any other purpose. "A room for two."

The woman moves behind the counter, heaves a large leather binder onto its surface, and flips it open.

"All right," she says. "A room for two? Two beds?"

Her eyes dart between Jason and myself behind him.

"I'm not with him," I blurt out. "I'm here with my grandma. She's waiting in the car."

"Yes," Jason quickly adds. "My friend and I were in an accident and these ladies were kind enough to give us a ride. My friend is also waiting outside."

The woman simply nods and flips to the next page in her binder. She spins the binder around to face Jason and places a pen on the page for him.

"If you'll sign in there," she says.

"Do you take cash, by chance?" Jason asks.

The woman grins, but it doesn't quite reach her eyes. I can already tell she's wary of him, picking up on exactly what I've picked up on during the last hour or so in the car: that he's an untrustworthy slime ball.

"It'll be an additional fifty-dollar deposit. You'll get that back when you check out tomorrow morning. One-hundred-and-seventy total for the room."

Jason freezes at the amount, perhaps caught off guard.

"Do you have that much?" I ask over his shoulder.

"Yeah," he says through his teeth. "I've got it."

He pulls his wallet from his back pocket and counts out several twenties, which he tosses onto the counter. Then he resumes signing in. I notice as the woman slides his cash off the counter, her eyes remain fixed on him, unblinking, until she begins operating the cash register under the counter where we can't see.

"You gonna ask about your friend's truck out there?" I say.

Hunched over the binder with the pen in his hand, Jason visibly stiffens to my words. I can't see his face very well where I'm standing, but I imagine he looks quite annoyed, which pleases me. A lot.

"Your friend's truck?" the woman says, as she places his change beside him. She furrows her brow.

I casually step to the side where I can better see Jason's face, his hesitation. After a speechless moment he offers the woman a phony smile which barely hides his impatience.

"There's a truck parked outside," he says. "It looks a lot like my buddy's truck, is all. Might be him, might not be. Though, it'd be very convenient if it was." He laughs and it sounds as forced as his smile looks. "You got a man by the name of Jasper staying the night, by chance?"

The woman behind the counter barely lifts an eyebrow. Her previously slitted eyes widen, but not by much.

"No Jaspers here, I'm afraid," she says.

Jason's smile crumbles, grimacing. "Hmm. That's a shame."

The woman turns and opens the cabinet on the wall, revealing a series of hooks inside, each with their own individual keys. She grabs one and places it on the binder where Jason is only now finishing up with his information. I glimpse the number on the keychain: 3.

"I lock up at eleven," the woman tells us. "But you're welcome to use the phone in your room to call should you need anything."

Jason grabs the keys, smiles fleetingly at the woman across the counter, then turns for the doors. As he passes me, from the corner of his mouth he mutters, "Thanks again for the ride, ma'am."

The bell jingles and he disappears. His use of 'ma'am' succeeds in irritating me, but my irritation is short-lived as I remind myself that this might be the last I ever see of him. *Good riddance.*

Now it's my turn. I approach the counter as the woman slides the pen toward me.

"Is it all right if I request a specific room?" I ask.

"Which one?"

"Sixteen, if it's available."

Judging by the near-vacant parking lot out back, I hazard a guess that it's available.

She turns to the cabinet of keys and retrieves Room 16's, which she places beside my arm as I hurriedly begin scratching in my information.

"Will you be paying with cash or card?"

"Card," I say.

The woman lifts a little card-reader device out from

under the counter and places it next to me when I'm ready. I insert my grandma's card and wait.

"Between the two of us, I'd keep an eye on that guy if I were you."

The woman quirks an eyebrow. "The one you arrived with? Why's that?"

The card reader beeps and tells me to remove my card. I stick it back into my coat pocket, then take up the pen again to finish signing in. I pause as I meet the woman eye to eye.

"I don't know," I tell her. "Let's just call it a feeling."

DARLENE

I watch through my side mirror—nearly obscured with frost—as Lana hurries toward the house, her white coat vanishing into the blowing snow like a figment.

It's just Carl and me now.

"How's your leg?" I ask him, mostly to fill the silence.

"My leg'll be all right," he says. He sighs gruffly. "Thanks again, by the way. It sure means a lot, you stopping for us like you did. I know I already said that, but…"

"Oh, don't even mention it. You were stranded in a blizzard, for crying out loud. Anyone else would have done the same. I apologize if my granddaughter comes across as a bit… reluctant. She doesn't trust anybody. It's all that nonsense she listens to. Those… *podcasts.*"

"She's smart." Carl says it with such a *sternness,* it surprises me. "I've only known you both for an hour or so, but I can already tell she's a clever one. I get the strong sense she understands people. Reads 'em well…"

"Oh?" Again I'm surprised. "What makes you say that?"

Carl is quiet for a moment. He shifts around some, clears his throat.

"That buddy of mine... or my *brother,* I should say..." He pauses again, giving me plenty of time to figure out what the hell *that* could mean. "Well... he's a bit of an asshole."

Carl laughs at what he's just said. I laugh at his candidness. I don't know how else to react. I think about those things I said before, about Lana and her questionable taste in men, and I'm beginning to regret having said them, truthfully.

"He might have jumped in front of your car, but your granddaughter spotted him from a mile away. I get the sense she's been around the block a few times. That's a girl who should continue trusting her instincts..."

Again, I'm not sure how to respond. It's dawning on me now, how I might have embarrassed Lana before by saying what I did. Carl's kindness shames me.

"I take it you and your... *brother*... don't get along too well?"

"Oh, he's fine," Carl says rather flippantly. "But I know who he really is... and he's not half the charmer he pretends to be."

My mind is abuzz with questions—my appetite for all things gossip and rumors positively whetted. I resist asking, however. I know Lana and Jason will return any minute, and it's none of my business, really.

"That's interesting..." I fold my hands into my lap and idly study the empty driver's seat beside me, as well as the cupholder between our seats stuffed with shoplifted Charleston Chews. "My granddaughter is the opposite. She can come across so *prickly* at times, and she's always been a handful, but… she's always had a good heart."

I gaze into the snow outside, literal *waves* of it flowing overhead above the motel roof.

"Well, ma'am, I can easily guess where she got it from," Carl says, bringing an unexpected smile to my face.

"Oh, who's the charmer now?"

Carl stirs in the backseat, which prompts me to peer in the direction of the Main Office where I see Jason approaching through the swirling snow.

"Looks like we've got our room," Carl says. "It was lovely meeting you, Darlene."

"You as well, Carl," I say, before Jason raps his knuckles on Carl's window.

Carl opens his door and hands one of their bags to Jason, followed by the other. Then he climbs out and shuts the door. Jason doesn't acknowledge me at all, not a glance or a wave or anything as he starts across the parking lot toward their room: Carl limps after him.

Now I'm alone.

I eye the Charleston Chews again, thinking on Carl's words.

I get the sense she's been around the block a few times…

Lana's lived a turbulent life, that's for sure. A lot of it wasn't even her fault. I wish things had been easier for her. I wish things were easier for her now. It certainly can't help having a grandmother who so easily loses sight of her struggles in light of the poor choices she sometimes makes.

Don't we all make poor choices sometimes? That's how we learn, after all.

I suppose I just wish she'd learn from some of those mistakes already, instead of endlessly repeating them.

I startle as the driver's door opens and Lana leans in, dangling a single key on its keychain before me.

"Room sixteen," she says, and nods to the door right in front of us.

She turns off the engine and pockets her car keys before popping the trunk open. I grab my purse and climb out into the bitter cold. I'm only standing outside for five seconds before I miss the warm heat blowing from the vents on my feet and my face. Lana carries our luggage bags out of the trunk, slams the trunk closed, and proceeds to drag our luggage through the snow to our door. I join her there, rubbing my hands to keep them warm.

"My *goodness*, it's cold out here..." I mutter.

She opens the door, gives it a push, and gestures for me to lead the way. I step inside and immediately search for the light switch on the wall. I flip it on. The ceiling light douses us in its bright, *cold* lighting. Like indoor moonlight. Unpleasant. There are two full-size beds against the wall, each with their own lamps on their nightstands. I twist the nearest lamp on, it's round lampshade illuminating with soft, warm amber light. Much better. I flick the ceiling light off as Lana steps back inside after having locked up the car. She shuts the door and locks it as well.

"Glad that's over with..." she says with a great, heavy sigh.

"Lana... about what I said before, in the car..." I pause, searching for my best words. Lana preemptively folds her arms, almost as if she were also expecting this, or possibly already thinking about it, too. "I shouldn't have said it. About you and your... *taste in men,* and the rest. That was inappropriate. I don't know what I was thinking. I'm sorry."

She smiles with one side of her mouth, frowns with the other, her eyes falling shut as she shrugs her shoulders.

"It's all right," she says, opening her eyes again and leveling them softly upon me. "I know you were only joking."

Except I don't think I was joking. And judging by the look in her eyes, she knows it. But she's forgiving me. So easily, too! It makes me feel that much more shame all over again.

"Well, it's not all right," I go on. "And that's why I wanted to apologize."

"Apology accepted," she says, and smiles with the rest of her mouth now. Even her gaze warms with it. She turns to the room, observing our sleeping quarters for the first time, taking it all in. "I'm guessing you want the bed closest to the bathroom?"

She winces as I plant a big wet kiss on her cheek, standing on my tiptoes to do it because she's a bit taller than I am.

"You know me so well," I say.

JASPER

*J*ennifer.

You're glowing today. I know that's cheesy to think, but it's true. You're actually *glowing*, and it's not just the golden hour, the way the setting sun lights us both on fire, but something else as well. You're so beautiful I can't stand it. How did a piece of shit like me get so lucky? I'll never know.

I put my hands around your waist and pull you against me, but there's something between us, something that doesn't let us stand as close as we used to, as I'd like to. But it's a miracle all its own. Another beauty. I slide my hands from off your waist and cup your swollen belly instead. I don't remember you being this far along before. Time flies, I guess. The sight of your body makes me giddy. Makes me anxious, too. I can't lie. I'm scared as hell. And I know that's rich. I'm not the one carrying this life form inside me, after all. I'm positive you must be scared, too, even if you don't seem to show it. I don't know how you do that. Aren't I supposed to be the strong one? The reliable one?

Then I feel it—something pressing back against me, against the palms of my hands. I look at you, and you can't help but laugh at the shock on my face.

"Her name is Gloria," you say, which is news to me, but it does feel right.

Everything in this moment feels right. Which is strange.

For a second I'm distracted by this feeling, this *off-ness,* and I look to your belly again where my hands are still cupped, where I can still feel Gloria kicking, and once again I wonder how I managed to get here.

No, really... how did I get here?

You place your hand upon my face and your touch electrifies me. You direct me to lift my gaze, to look you in the eye once more. You're still smiling, but in a gentle way. Still glowing, too. Then you place your other hand upon my face, so that you're holding me like I'm holding your belly, and you pull me in, pull my lips to yours and kiss me. Your kiss is sweet but unexpected. Different.

How did I get here?

You kiss me harder still. Your wet tongue slips between my lips, into my mouth, and while I'm surprised I'm not opposed. I close my eyes and kiss you back. I slide my hands to your waist again as you press yourself to me, your mouth never leaving mine as your hands push themselves up my face, into my hair, grasping me, kissing harder, your tongue more forceful.

When I open my eyes again everything is dark.

Or darker than it was.

I'm lying down and you're on top of me. Your tongue is still in my mouth even though I'm not moving at all, and suddenly... suddenly...

Suddenly…

You pull away from me, your face softly lit by the light coming through the doorway of this strange room.

You're not Jennifer.

I turn my face away. I can't move much else. My head feels heavy as a cannonball. My torso, my limbs, they're all full of lead that holds me still, renders me immobile. You… no, the woman on top of me… continues trying to kiss me, tries to turn my face toward her again, but I simply turn the other way.

"Stop," I'm barely able to say. My voice is slurred. Drunken. "Stop… you're not…"

"No, no, no," the woman whispers breathily into my ear. "Go back to sleep now…"

I want to push her away but I can't fucking move. She kisses me on the cheek. Once, twice, inching closer to my mouth which I can't turn any farther away before she's abruptly interrupted by a series of piercing, brassy *dings* from elsewhere in the house. A ringing bell. She finally stops. She sits upright, her weight lifting from my chest, allowing me to get a full breath of air for the first time since waking.

"Who the hell could that be…" she murmurs irritably under her breath. She looks at me, her face partially obscured in shadow. "Go back to sleep, okay?"

I want to scream. Because this isn't normal. Something is wrong. With me. With her. I want to scream but my voice won't cooperate. My jaw won't cooperate. I want to sit up, to climb out of this bed, but my body won't cooperate, either. I've never felt so *heavy* in my life. It reminds me of the times I've gotten *too* stoned. *Couch lock.* Some people don't mind it, I guess. I mind it. I mind it very much. I can't move.

She leaves the room and shuts the door behind her. A moment later I hear voices. Their words are unintelligible. I will myself to roll, to fall out of this bed, to make a ruckus. This isn't right. None of this is right. Why was she on top of me? Why was her tongue in my mouth? Why can't I move or speak?

Drugged. I've been drugged. Obviously.

For a moment I try to consider the possibility that this is simply related to my injuries, that I've lost too much blood and therefore my faculties have diminished, too. But no. This is more than that. This is worse than that. Somehow. My thoughts are messy and I can't figure out *how* this is worse yet, but my instincts are telling me so. Just like the one on the counter downstairs, my warning bells are *ringing*.

I'm in danger here.

I lay in a panic for a few minutes before the bedroom door opens. She's returned. She leaves the door open as she strolls toward me. She turns on the lamp on the nightstand next to me, illuminating us both. There's a certain sort of panic in her eyes as well. She looks me over, meets my gaze.

"You need to rest," she says.

She takes up the bowl of soup still sitting on its tray on the nightstand. That's it, I realize. The source. She sits beside me with the bowl in her hands, and attempts to bring a spoonful of it toward my face.

"Open wide," she says, her voice instilled with great kindness that doesn't at all match what I *know* to be the truth, what's *really* going on here. "Open, open, open..."

I turn my face away. I've got strength enough for that and not much else.

My voice barely *ekes* out of my mouth. *"No..."*

"Just a little bit," she says.

The spoon touches the corner of my mouth and it's not even warm anymore. How much time has passed? How long have I been lying in this bed?

"To help you sleep..."

"No," I say again.

Then her hand is on my face. She turns me toward her forcefully, my chin clamped between her thumb and index, and she tries to open my mouth. I'm not able to resist her. She spoons the soup into my mouth. I will my throat to close and I choke on it. I splutter. Soupy spittle mists the air and she recoils from me.

"Damn you," she says, and angrily returns the spoon into the bowl, clinking noisily. "That's no way to behave."

She stands upright, towering over me. The lamp casts it light along her face from underneath so that she's transformed into a kind of nightmarish version of herself. I'd be lying if I said I wasn't afraid of her then. More afraid than I already was. She looks down her nose at me, hands on her hips.

"Get some sleep," she says, her voice quavering. "You need it."

She leaves me alone once more, turning off the lamp before she goes. She steps into the hall and shuts the door behind her.

Dark as a tomb.

QUENTIN

*S*omehow I'm both stunned and unsurprised at finding my truck parked outside this shitty little motel. I'm stunned by the absurdity of it. I'm unsurprised that an idiot like Jasper would take his chances here.

But he is here, without a doubt.

With the light off, I stand at our motel room window with the curtain discreetly pulled aside, peering out into the snowy parking lot, toward the house with its downstairs lights all on, it's upstairs lights all off. Our room—Room 3 —is directly under the lamppost on this side of the parking lot. I don't think it's a coincidence. I think the motel manager put us here because she knows something. Or suspects something. She must have already gotten a good look at Jasper when he arrived. Anyone could make a whole host of assumptions about a guy like him—a nervous, fidgety, dumb-as-a-doornail weasel like him. So if someone shows up shortly after claiming to know the truck he arrived in, naturally you might start making similar assumptions about them, too. Bad company, etcetera, etcetera…

She put us in Room 3 underneath the working lamppost in order to keep an eye on us through the night. Across the parking lot, behind the house, is another lamppost like the one outside our window, except that one's flickering off and on like it's about to go kaput any second.

I study the house itself. The *Main Office.* I gaze toward those upstairs windows and can sense someone looking back. She's up there now, I think, watching.

I'm not in an entirely sour mood, however. I know Jasper is here, which means he didn't make off with our boss' money. Not yet. That's good news.

I also know that he's staying in Room 19. I noticed when the manager fetched our room key from her little cabinet behind the counter that only one other key was missing. Room 19's key. There are only twenty rooms at this quaint establishment. Now it's only a matter of waiting. Biding my time. Picking the perfect moment to strike and take back what's mine.

You stupid prick.

I gaze across the parking lot toward the back half of the motel, toward the last stretch of rooms at its end. The second-to-last door should be his. There's no way I can just sneak over there now, however. Not with the manager likely watching. Not with that light perpetually shining on our doorstep. I'll have to wait.

Or find another way.

Over my shoulder, across the room, the bathroom door stands open with the light on inside. Allen's in there now— or should I say *Carl*—cleaning himself up after our little winter storm altercation. I cross the room, chewing the inside of my cheek as I consider my options. In the bathroom doorway, I find Allen sitting on the lip of the bathtub inside, his pants discarded on the bathroom floor. He's rinsing his leg under the hot water, swirling pink with blood down the drain. He notices me watching and gives me a cursory glance.

"The bullet's still in me," he says. "I've got nothing to dig it out with…"

"You look through Jasper's bag? Or the emergency bag?"

"No, not yet. I'll take a look in a minute…" He winces as he places the gunshot wound directly under the steaming hot water. "Fuck…"

"We know he's here," I say, thinking my thoughts out loud. I lean against the doorframe.

"And?" Allen grimaces, hisses through his teeth. "What are we doing about it?"

Continuing to chew my cheek, I draw my gaze over Allen's pathetic, half-naked self, then along the back wall of the bathroom where a window sits over the toilet, looking out over the fields behind the motel. The windowpane's glass is clear, but it's slightly frosted from the blowing snow that's gathered on the other side.

"Hmm."

I leave Allen to his business for a moment. I take the emergency roadside kit and plop it onto the end of one of the beds, where I begin rummaging through its contents. I pull out a flashlight. I click the orange rubber button and it shines bright. Good as new. I stick it into my jacket pocket. Then I pull the pillowcase off the pillow on the bed, stuff it into my jacket pocket, and return into the bathroom. I straddle the toilet and flick the plastic lever that locks the window in place. With my palm flat against the glass, it's a struggle to slide it open at first, but once it starts to move, it *moves.* I jerk it fully open. Cold wind rushes in. Snow flecks my face, sends goosebumps up my arms.

"What are you doing?" Allen asks, twisting around on the lip of the tub, wobbling, nearly falling onto the floor as he does it. The idiot.

"I'm gonna go check on our friend. When you're done with… whatever you're doing… do me a favor and keep an eye on the truck outside. In case I manage to flush him out."

With that, I stand up onto the toilet, the loose lid sliding around under my boots. The window is pretty small—too small for a man my size, I would wager, but I intend to squeeze through anyway. I put one leg through into the bitter cold. My pant leg rides up, my ankle freezing. Then I hunch myself down, duck my head through, and proceed to pull myself the rest of the way out until I jump sloppily into the snow below the window.

With the cold wind howling in my ears, I begin making my way around the backside of the motel.

MISSY

I'm standing in our dark bedroom peering out our window, watching the motel down below. Watching Room 3, to be exact. These are the men responsible for Jasper's injuries. His pursuers. Perhaps the owners of all that money, as well. They know he's here. Should I have moved his truck? Hidden it somewhere? I'd assumed it was hidden enough parked out back like it is, but apparently not. I wouldn't have expected them to stop by.

What kind of accident were they in, I wonder, that resulted in needing to hitch a ride with strangers? I repeat the young woman's advice, wondering what she knows, or what she *thinks* she knows.

I'd keep an eye on that guy if I were you…

Well, naturally. I plan to do just that. They know their friend is here somewhere. However, not only do they not know which room is his, they don't know he's not even in his room, but in here with me. Should push come to shove, they would be wise to keep their distance.

I'm not afraid to defend myself.

I leave the window and cross to the second window over our bed. This window gives me a nice overhead view of the back lot, rooms 11 through 20. Except tonight it's a little hard to see, what with all the frost and snowflakes sticking to the window screen. I can see the light on in Room 16's window, where the women stay. Room 19's window is dark, just as I left it. I can also look straight down to the row of parking spots behind the house, to the truck parked there. It's locked up. I checked. There should be no funny business tonight without my knowing about it.

Nobody sneaks around this place without my knowing about it.

Not even you.

I take a seat on the edge of the bed, where I eye the bottom drawer of my nightstand. I find myself thinking about those pictures on his phone again. The raunchy ones. Just the thought of them burns me up inside. Burns me up sick. I don't want to think about those pictures anymore, but they keep forcing their way into my mind's eye, along with other images from long ago—memories from long ago. It frightens me, how they blur together. The images and the memories, as well as the thoughts and feelings they conjure. I loathe this feeling. These *feelings*. Like I want to love somebody, to touch somebody, to *hurt* somebody...

Control yourself.

I remember when we ran this motel together. I remember...

I remember too much, to be honest. I wish I could forget already. I wish I could just forget about *all of that* without also forgetting you. Forgetting you is the last thing I want to do.

Your wool sweater still lies piled at the foot of our bed where I left it. I stretch for it, snatch it up. I bring it to my face once again and bury myself in it, inhaling it. It doesn't smell like you, though. Not anymore. I take your sweater into the hallway, into the bathroom across the hall where I grab a bottle of your cologne from under the sink. You never used this particular bottle. It's newer than that. But it's your scent. I give the sweater a couple sprays. Then, standing in our dark bathroom, I bury my face into the green wool once more and inhale. Tears spring to my eyes. It's your scent, but it's not *your* scent.

It's the best I can do. Unless…

I step into the hallway. I look from our bedroom doorway to the closed door at the end of the hall where *he* sleeps. I head there, then pause just outside, your sweater in my hands. The scent of your cologne lingers in my nostrils. I open the door, but I'm quiet about it.

"Jasper?" I whisper.

There's no response. I open the door fully, letting in the light from the hallway. It's enough to see him by. His eyes are closed, his face slack. He's asleep, as he should be. I turn on the bedside lamp and then wait a moment. The brighter light doesn't wake him. He's still heavily sedated. The only reason he woke before was because I'd gotten carried away, I think.

I scrunch your sweater up, with my hands widening the neck hole as I carefully pull it over his sleeping head. Then I maneuver him into it, pushing his limp arms into the arms of the sweater, one by one, before finally pulling it the rest of the way down his torso.

Am I getting carried away again?

I circle the foot of the bed to the other side, where I draw the covers down and slip in beside him. His eyes are still closed, his mouth slightly parted. I put my ear beside his lips and listen to his soft breaths. I feel them, too, warm and humid against me. The whole bed is warm, cooking with his body heat. I scoot myself closer. I slip my arm beneath his pillow, beneath his head, then rest mine upon his chest, upon the soft wool of your old sweater. I wriggle my body even closer to his, as close as our bodies can be. I inhale deeply, breathe him in. I breathe *you* in. Your scent and his intertwine more beautifully than I could have imagined. I hold that breath for a long moment before letting it out, and with it I feel so much tension slip out of me likewise. My shoulders relax. My *everything* relaxes. I take another breath, let it out slow, then sigh pleasantly, snuggled up against the both of you. It's better than I'd hoped. It's practically perfect.

It's like we're together again.

LANA

*M*y phone doesn't get a signal out here, which is crazy to me. Is it the storm? Is it that this motel is biblical purgatory? I don't know. But I do have several unread text messages I must have received in the last hour, which I eagerly scroll through as my grandma spends the next ten minutes in the bathroom getting ready for bed.

Ninety-percent of these texts are from *him*. Daniel. The most recent of them reads: *I bet a whore like u doesn't even care.* The text before that reads: *karma's a bitch, bitch.* And the text before that reads: *Carter has herpes btw. did u even know?*

Carter is Daniel's best friend, whom Daniel believes I've slept with in order to get back at him for his betrayal. Multiple betrayals, actually. It's funny to me that he would make up such a lie about his best friend just to scare me, considering he's more likely to have contracted something from the multiple Tinder hookups he pursued while we were together. It doesn't matter to me, anyway, because I never actually slept with Carter.

And to be perfectly honest besides, if I had to choose I'd take herpes over Daniel any day after what he did to me.

He doesn't even know the worst of what he's done.

I turn my phone off entirely, set it on the nightstand by my bed, and lay back on my pillow while I wait for my grandma to wrap up her bedtime routine. I'll start mine when she finishes.

Even with my phone powered off, however, I can't stop thinking about Daniel—his texts, our relationship, and what a waste of two years that was. Or the fact that he doesn't even know...

Stop. Stop thinking about it.

I can't stop thinking about it. *The nonsense.* Because it's more than that. I'm not being honest with myself when I call it that. It's my attempt to diminish the gravity of the situation. Nonsense can be ignored, and this *does not* fit the criteria.

I know I should tell Daniel—that he should suffer the anxiety the same as me—but telling him only makes the situation *more real*, and I don't want it to be real. I want it to be over.

You did this to yourself.

Was my grandma right before? About my taste in men? I can admit my past partners have been duds, but after so many missteps, so many duds, I have to fess up eventually, don't I? I'm not innocent in this. The pattern exists for a reason.

She's got a broken picker, is the problem. The absolute worst taste in men, hands down...

It's harsh, but I think she's right. Thanks, Grandma.

...it's nothing to do with the genes that obviously run in your family, I can tell you that...

Jason's words assault me unexpectedly. My face twists into an involuntary scowl as I hear his voice in my head. He was trying to get on my nerves when he said that, I know, but the words stung me in a way I'm sure he was oblivious to. The words *still* sting, actually.

A lot more runs in my family than genes, I think.

I have the memories to prove it.

Finally my grandma steps out of the bathroom. She's in her silk pajamas, her face freshly moisturized. She sighs pleasantly on her way to her bed, where she pulls the covers down and begins inspecting the sheets.

"Grandma," I say. "How old were you when you had my mom?"

She thinks about it for a moment. "Twenty-six. Why?"

I can't help staring at my phone again, sitting dark on my nightstand. My stomach does somersaults.

"No reason." Then, in an effort to drastically change the subject, I ask, "What are your thoughts on revenge?"

It's a silly question. A careless question. I'm mostly asking to be entertained and, again, to change the subject.

"Revenge?" she says, as she bends down close to study her bedding. "It's just a waste of everyone's time, I think. Why make one wrong into two..." She straightens, apparently satisfied by her inspection. She levels her eyes on me, considering my question more seriously now. "Why? Are you picking at scabs?"

"No," I lie. "Of course not."

She gives me that funny smile of hers, when she knows I'm bullshitting but finds me so incredibly endearing.

"Leave that man be, Lana," she says. She has such a magical way of cutting straight to the heart of the matter. "Cheaters don't deserve a second thought. Do yourself a favor and just *leave... him... be...*"

I let out a heavy sigh of my own as I swivel myself off the bed and spring to my feet.

"A little late for that, I'm afraid," I mutter.

I open my luggage case on the floor at the foot of my bed while my grandma climbs under the covers, settling in. I pull out a few of my bathroom items, as well as my own oversized pajama shirt for sleeping. As I stand up with these things, my grandma stops me.

"It's freezing in here," she says. "Don't you think it's freezing in here?"

Her eyes are wandering over her bedding, like it's not enough. I set down my things and locate the room's thermostat on the wall. It appears to be set at seventy degrees Fahrenheit. I toggle it slightly and wait. Nothing changes. I don't hear anything coming on. I toggle it some more, but there's still no change.

"Hmm. This doesn't seem to do anything."

"Do you think it's cold?" my grandma asks. "Or is it just me?"

"No, yeah, it's cold," I agree. "I'm guessing these rooms are all controlled by a master thermostat or something? I have no clue..."

"Well, I'll probably be all right. It's only for one night. I can even put some extra layers on, I suppose..."

"No. I'll go ask the manager about it. If nothing else, maybe they've got some extra blankets."

"Oh, don't go bothering them. It's so late as it is..."

"Grandma, I'm sorry, but if they don't want to be bothered at night, they've chosen the wrong industry. Besides, it's still not eleven yet. The doors should still be open."

I put my puffy white coat back on, along with my boots which I previously kicked off by the door. I pull my hood onto my head and, with my hair sticking wildly out around my face, I give my grandma a funny look, knowing full well what a goofy mess I am.

"I'll be back," I say with my best—and still terrible—Schwarzenegger impression.

The wind is still roaring overhead as I step outside, carrying great white puffs of snow with it. I'm not sure if it's still actually snowing or if the wind is simply carrying old snow back into the air from the rooftops. I stick my hands into my coat pockets and hurry across the parking lot, careful not to slip on the icy asphalt. I make my way to the front of the house again, lit up like a red-light-district brothel from the towering roadside sign.

The 11th Hour Motel.

I briefly reflect on the fact that I'm hurrying toward the house's entrance, trying to beat the clock before it's 11 PM. Except my little inside joke doesn't even make sense, really, considering 11 PM technically marks the twenty-third hour, not the eleventh.

Whatever.

The bell over the door jingles once again as I push inside. I stroll into the middle of the front room—I guess what you'd call the *lobby*—and wait a moment, hoping someone's heard the bell. Is it only the woman, I wonder? I can't help thinking what an unsafe business this would be to run *alone*, let alone as a single woman.

No one's coming. I'll have to ring the bell on the counter. Unlike the asshole before me, however, I ring it twice. Only twice. It's loud and it's clear and, most importantly, it's enough.

Or so I tell myself.

Still no one comes.

I wander to the edge of the counter, toward the hallway. At the other end, the kitchen light is on.

"Hello?"

I proceed cautiously down the hallway, and as I do, a very specific part of my brain is triggered—the part that enjoys doing things I know I shouldn't. I'm in forbidden territory now, and my entire body *thrills* at the prospect.

Obviously there's something wrong with me.

"Hello?" I call again.

I pause as I reach the first doorway on my left. The living room. It's mostly dark except for the television, where it appears the owner was in the middle of watching a movie. The screen is dimmed, but I can still make out the image. A man in the desert. The actor's name escapes me, but I know my grandma loves him.

I continue into the kitchen. The light is on, but no one's in here, either. I notice the wash bucket from earlier is now sitting on the counter beside the kitchen sink. The small round table to my left is bare except for a duffel bag sitting at its edge. I look over my shoulder, peering toward the other end of the hallway where I started, making sure I'm actually alone. I don't hear footsteps or any movement upstairs, either. No one's coming. Not yet.

I saunter to the edge of the table, to the duffel bag sitting so innocuously there.

Not only am I a bit of a thief, I must confess I'm also a notorious snooper. Between me and my grandma's penchant for gossip, we're a dangerous duo, for sure.

The bag is already unzipped. With a single pull of my finger, I open it wide.

My breath catches in my throat.

Holy Mother of God.

The bag is full of money. Cash. Moolah. Bundles of one-hundred-dollar bills. The sight of it is so entirely alien to me, my brain short circuits. If the goal of meditation is to clear your mind, I'm a certified Zen master for at least five seconds as I stare into the bag. I don't know what to think. My jaw is *dropped.*

"Oh my god," I mutter.

I cast another glance over my shoulder, toward the hall-way. I step away from the table, peering toward the front of the house, ensuring once again that no one is coming, that no one is about to get the jump on me as I do possibly one of the stupidest things I've ever done in my life.

I return to the bag on the table. I pull it open and marvel all over again. Whose money is this? It can't be the manager's, I think. Why would she keep a bag of money like this sitting open in plain sight? Where did she get this? Where did it come from?

Without any plausible answer I can think of, I let impulse guide me. Perhaps greed, too. Before my reeling mind can even catch up with the reality of this situation, my hands are reaching into the bag, grasping those beautiful bundles of green in my fists. I stuff them into my coat pockets. Two bundles. Four bundles. Six bundles. I think I stop at ten bundles, five in each pocket, but I'm not sure.

I'm not actually counting. Everything is a blur. It seems there's a squash match taking place in my chest, my heart is slamming so rapidly.

This is a lot more than some gas station candy, to say the least.

I regard what's left in the bag. Plenty. I definitely took enough to be noticed, however. A considerable amount. A chunk of change, as they say. I quickly reach inside and rearrange the bundles so that they're flush. Then I shut the bag again—or pull it closed so that you can't readily see its contents.

With my pockets full, I hurry back into the lobby, making a beeline for the front door before I remember why I came here in the first place. I screech to a halt with my hand outstretched for the doorknob.

"Shit."

I turn to face the counter once more. I can't leave empty handed—at least, not in the way of blankets. I hate the thought of returning to my grandma without them as much as I hate the idea of her shivering all night long. I grit my teeth, annoyed with myself for making things so complicated.

"Hello?" I call out, extra loudly this time.

I approach the front counter and tap the bell numerous times like an asshole. Because I *am* an asshole. That's the truth, isn't it? They say we hate in others what we recognize in ourselves. That would honestly explain so much if it were true. I hate loads of people.

"Hello?"

Finally I hear movement. Footsteps. I stand back and peer toward the head of the staircase. She appears there again. The woman in charge. Instead of wiping her mouth, this time she's wiping sleep from her eyes. I obviously woke her.

"Sorry to bother you," I lie.

"No, that's all right…" She stops at the top of the staircase with her hand on the rail. "I dozed off. Is there something I can do for you?"

"I was just wondering if you happened to have some extra blankets. The thermostat doesn't seem to work in our room…"

"Oh. I'm so sorry. Yes. Of course…"

The woman pivots back into the upstairs hallway and is gone momentarily. I hear what sounds like a closet door opening, closing, and then the shuffle of footsteps returning to the stairs. She emerges once more, this time with her arms full of blankets. A stack of three, by the looks of them. It's more than we need, but I don't want to waste any more time in this place. I meet her at the bottom stair, where she hands them into my arms. I burn with shame and paranoia, as I pray the money in my pockets stays put. With the stack of blankets balanced against myself, I fear they'll squeeze a stray bundle of cash out of my pocket like a slippery bar of soap onto the floor.

"Was that everything?"

The woman pulls her long, sandy hair over one shoulder, then folds her arms under her breasts, still blinking her groggy eyes.

"Yes, thank you," I say, turning for the door. "This is perfect. Thank you, thank you…"

She follows me, her footsteps trailing at my heels.

"Let me get the door for you," she says.

I thank her once again. My heart is still pounding. She pulls the door open and I slip outside into the freezing storm, with my arms full of wobbly blankets. I thank her one last time over my shoulder but the closing door interrupts me, followed by the loud *knock* of the deadbolt turning into place.

QUENTIN

*F*uck, it's cold. I can't stop reminding myself that I should be at home right now, curled up in a blanket watching *Bob's Burgers* reruns with Marston. Marston's my Dachshund. He gets lonely without me, but sometimes there's nothing I can do. Work is work. Somebody's got to pay the bills.

Somebody's got to take out the trash.

That's exactly what I intend to do when I find him. Jasper. I wonder if he knows we're here already, if he spied us in the parking lot after we arrived. He's got to be paranoid, at least. Probably won't be getting a wink of sleep tonight. I imagine the little rat getting out of bed repeatedly to peer outside his window into the stormy parking lot, waiting for our dark figures to come knocking. I hope he doesn't expect us to come from behind. He should. Any intelligent person would, but luckily that's not what I'm dealing with tonight.

I turn the corner of the motel, making my way along the rear length of the L as snow broadsides me from across the surrounding field. The sky is mostly dark. I can only faintly make out the fluffy underbellies of the clouds overhead, through the thick, slanting snowfall. Will this storm ever let up, I wonder?

I trace the length of the building until I come to the final two windows, marking the final two rooms. Jasper should be in the second to last. Room 19. I stop at that window. I click on my flashlight. Using my jacket sleeve, I swipe away as much snow as I can that's gathered on the glass. Then I stand on tiptoe, giving me a good enough angle to peer fully into the bathroom—enough that my flashlight reveals Jasper's discarded jacket on the bathroom floor.

Bingo.

Unfortunately, there's no way for me to infiltrate his room with subtlety. He's going to know I'm coming one way or another. I realize what a mistake I've made, leaving Allen responsible for keeping an eye on things from the other side. That bum-legged dumbass couldn't chase after a cockroach let alone this vermin.

I have to consider possibilities. Jasper could still be armed. Probably he is. What I'd really like to do is kick in the front door, but I'm afraid I'll draw the motel manager's attention doing that, and then I'll have the police to contend with. This is the best I can do without staking out his room all night hoping he'll come out on his own.

I pray he's asleep. If he's not, I hope I'm able to do this faster than he's able to roll himself out of bed and grab his gun.

It's now or never.

I turn off my flashlight. I pull the pillowcase from my pocket, fold it lengthwise, and quickly tie it around the elbow of my coat sleeve for some extra protection. I elbow the window, hard. A bigger piece of glass breaks out than I expect. It falls to the floor inside, smaller bits raining onto the bathroom tile. I elbow another good portion out of the window frame. I have to move fast. I take out my pistol, quickly use the barrel to break the remaining glass out of the window frame, and proceed to hoist myself through the opening and into the bathroom.

It's much too late for such realizations, but I realize how fucking stupid this whole plan is as I stumble clumsily onto the toilet underneath the window, nearly pitching myself face first into the bathtub. This isn't a plan at all. This is desperation. I've only tricked myself into believing otherwise.

I catch myself against the edge of the bathtub, force myself upright, standing straight with my gun in both hands aimed into the open doorway, shaking and gasping because I'm also not in nearly as good of shape as I like to tell myself.

Nothing happens.

There's no movement—no limbs sliding across bedsheets or footsteps drawing up against the wall outside the bathroom doorway. Nothing.

Slowly, cautiously, I step toward the doorway. My eyes are gradually adjusting to the dark. A tiny piece of glass crunches under my boot and I stop. I hold my breath to listen. Jasper's jacket lays at my feet on the tile. I crouch slightly, pick it up, and give it a little toss into the room. It plops onto the floor.

Nothing happens.

"Jasper?" I say in a low voice.

I move into the doorway. I lean ever so carefully into the room, studying the shadows with my gun at the ready. The shadows themselves remain empty and still. Nothing charges me. No one breathes but me.

The room is empty.

The fuck?

I take out my flashlight, click it on, and swipe its bright beam from one corner to the next, across the singular bed. There's nobody here. But that *is* Jasper's jacket, I'm certain. I train my light on it, where I tossed it onto the carpet, and reveal the dried blood I hadn't noticed in the dark.

Jasper was bleeding. Badly.

Then it hits me: the wash bucket inside the woman's home. She'd been scrubbing something from the carpet, hadn't she? Was it...

Was it you, Jasper boy?

He's not in here, but he was. I think it's unlikely he decided to switch rooms and left his bloody jacket behind. No, something else happened. I think I know where he is. I think the motel manager knows a thing or two as well.

No Jaspers here, I'm afraid...

Sneaky, sneaky. She's protecting him. Or he's already dead and she's protecting herself. Either way, she was expecting us and this could get a whole lot messier if we're not careful.

I conduct one more quick sweep of the room before I grab Jasper's jacket off the floor and head for the bathroom window. I climb back outside. Back into the cold. I skirt the rear of the motel once again, in reverse this time. I toss the jacket through our room's bathroom window and proceed to climb back in. It's not a pretty sight, me pulling myself in and over. Once more I'm out of breath. I take a seat on top of the toilet lid for a moment, collecting myself, before I slide the window shut and take Jasper's jacket into the room where I find Allen fast asleep on one of the beds.

"You fucking moron," I say aloud, which he doesn't hear. It doesn't rouse him in the slightest. So instead I toss Jasper's bloody jacket directly onto Allen, which startles a shout from him. "Nice job keeping an eye out."

"Huh?" he says, throwing the jacket off himself and onto the floor. He looks around, confused. "Oh. Sorry. I sat down for a second, and I—"

"I don't care. Do you see that?" I point to the jacket on the floor he so carelessly swept aside.

"The jacket?"

"It's his. I found it in his room. Except he's not there."

Allen furrows his brow, eyeing the jacket. I can see his two brain cells trying to friction together a flame in that thick skull of his.

"Is that—"

"It's blood," I answer. "We must have got him pretty good..."

I cross to the window and pull the curtain aside, enough to peek out into the parking lot. Everything is a cold wash of wind and snow, but I can make out the young woman from before departing the Main Office. She's carrying an armful of what looks like bedding. Blankets. *Lana* was her name, I remind myself. I track her through the storm all the way back to her room.

"He may or may not be alive," I go on. "But that woman —the one who runs the motel—knows for sure. She's keeping secrets. And I intend to find out what they are."

DARLENE

$\mathcal{I}$'ve always hated to be a bother, but it really is cold. And Lana's better about these things than I am. Being a bother, I mean. She's never afraid to ruffle feathers or state her business. She's never been a pushover. She's good at getting what she wants, one way or another.

Which for me has always begged the question—why doesn't that girl want more for herself?

She's a mystery to me. An enigma. I'll probably never fully understand her. But I do appreciate her.

I shiver as I await her return. Sitting on my bed, I rub my hands together like a fly, trying to warm them. My hands are always the coldest. I eye the useless thermostat on the wall. Seems typical in a place like this, doesn't it? I wouldn't be surprised if the plastic thermostat was just that —plastic on the wall.

Pretty soon I hear her outside the door, fumbling with the doorknob. I'm about to stand when the door opens. She gives it a push, making room for herself as her arms are clearly full. Like the Charleston Chews, she's come back to me with much more than I asked for. She kicks the door shut behind herself, brings the stack of blankets to the foot of my bed, and drops them there in a dramatic show of effort.

"Before you say anything, I didn't ask for all of these," she says, noticing the look on my face. "This is just what she gave me."

"Well... maybe I'll take a couple, anyway. It *is* freezing in here. Don't you think it's freezing?"

"It is," she agrees.

She remains standing at the foot of my bed. She sticks her hands into her coat pockets, chewing her lip like she's thinking deeply about something. Distracted. Her eyes wander from the toppled blankets to the door.

"Are you going to take one, at least?" I ask.

She nods suddenly, remembering herself. She grabs one of the three blankets and tosses it onto her bed nearer the door. Then she stops again, watching the door, glancing to her luggage on the floor, then back to the door.

"Did you forget something?"

She lets out a deep breath. "No, I just..." She shakes her head, as if to rid what's distracting her. She begins reaching awkwardly around in her coat pocket, as if it's full of trinkets, until she happens upon what she wants and pulls it out. I immediately recognize a new, unopened pack of cigarettes.

"I'm gonna step outside for a minute," she says.

"In this cold? In this blizzard?"

She starts for the door, but glances over her shoulder as she goes and says, "I've smoked through worse."

"You should really get a handle on these bad habits of

yours," I say, letting my mouth speak before my mind fully weighs the meaning of the words. "These things don't serve you, Lana."

"Yeah, well…"

Then the door is open and she's already slipped out. She shuts the door behind her and everything is eerily silent once again. I sit for a moment, wondering about that girl, before I finally stand and start unfolding my new blankets. I lay them out across the entire bed, two additional blankets, one on top of the other. Should be nice and heavy and warm to lay under. Once I'm satisfied, I pull the covers back and begin climbing in before I stop myself. I look to my own luggage on the floor. There's something in there I'd really like to look at—something I'm certain will help me sleep easier tonight with it beside my bed.

I kneel beside my luggage bag and lift the lid open, and right away I'm faced with it, nestled into my clothes like a sleeping babe.

The entire purpose of this trip of ours.

I take the urn into my hands—brushed nickel—and as I turn it upright, I can feel my husband's remains settling inside. Ashes to ashes, dust to dust, and all that. Some might think it morbid, but keeping him close has been a comfort to me—a comfort I'm finally letting go, as per his wishes. If I leave this mortal coil without fulfilling this one promise, I just know I'll be hearing about it for all of eternity—that is, if an afterlife even exists.

For my sake, I hope it does.

LANA

$\mathcal{I}$ can barely hide my anxiety. My grandma sees it, no doubt. It's not just anxiety, either. I'm still feeling the *rush*, the adrenaline, as well as the uncertain euphoria of literally lining my pockets with so much cash.

The adrenaline only starts wearing off after I've fetched my lighter from the car, lit a cigarette from my freshly opened pack, and taken my first long drag. I stand just outside our motel room door, under the overhanging roof where the snow blows over us in sheets. A ceiling of white. I let out my first breath of cigarette smoke. I watch it plume before me, warm and full of chemicals, and feel so much stress leave my body with it. I needed this. I needed this badly, as bad as it might be for me. It was impulsive of me to take that money, I know. Risky as hell. Sometimes I don't know when to say when. I'm fully aware of that.

I gaze toward the other half of the motel, stretching toward the road. I study Room 3 specifically, practically centered underneath the lamppost there. Then, just as I look away, movement draws my attention right back. It's him.

Jason. Through the slanted snow, shoulders hunched, hands jammed into his pockets, he moves hastily across the parking lot toward the manager's home. He vanishes around the corner. *Good luck,* I think, knowing the manager's already locked her doors. Maybe he called ahead already. She said we could do that.

I take another long drag.

Now there's a light on upstairs, in the motel manager's home. Possibly her bedroom light? I imagine she's getting ready for bed, and swearing like a sailor as that piece of shit pounds on her front door. Is he cold, too, I wonder? Has he come to ask for extra blankets? I hope she's all out, that we took everything she had. Let him shiver his ass off.

You should really get a handle on these bad habits of yours…

I take another drag to smooth the edges of my grandma's words.

As I stand under the relative safety and shadow of the motel, and watch the blowing snow whip overhead, I'm reminded of another time like this. Another trip, another storm. Years ago. I'd been with my mom then, when she was still around…

Although that hadn't been a snowstorm, but a tropical one. Wet and windy and violent. We'd just been evicted from our apartment in Florida, about a month after my dad vanished like a thief in the night with everything we had. I can still remember that weekend. I was only six then. I guess that hadn't been so much of a trip as it was a mandatory relocation. We couldn't afford rent, let alone a decent room for the night, so we'd stayed in a motel not so different from this one. My mom had said that merely finding a new place wasn't good enough, that we needed to get *as far away as possible* in order to escape the drama my dad had left in his wake.

Somehow the drama always managed to follow us, though. Wherever we went.

Something across the parking lot catches my eye, interrupting my faraway brooding. The light in the upstairs window. It flashes, changes position, as if a lamp has just fallen over. Curious, I step forward, blowing another cloud of smoke from the corner of my mouth. I watch that window intently, its light all crooked and wrong against the blinds. Has something just happened? An accident?

Worse?

Jason just went over there, I remind myself. He hasn't left yet, as far as I can tell.

Is something wrong?

Is the motel manager in trouble?

I'm about to take another step forward, to begin making my way across the parking lot in order to check on things, to check on *her,* when suddenly the light in the window rights itself, and this time I can clearly tell that a lamp has just been placed back where it belongs, having fallen somehow.

Then a shadow presses against the window blinds, pulls the blinds apart. A face peers out. I retreat reflexively, stepping back into the shadows. Even at a distance and through the snow, I can see that the shadow in the window is hers. The woman's. She must be okay.

An accident then, I think.

At last she steps away from the window, and nothing follows.

Unless I missed him somehow, I still haven't seen Jason

return to his room. I did get a little distracted, admittedly, reminiscing like I was. Maybe he slipped by. Either way, I finish my cigarette before dropping it to the snow at my feet and smushing it with my boot.

Then I head inside.

MISSY

I lock the door behind the young woman and pray that's all for tonight. No more visits. No more interruptions. It's almost 11pm, anyway. If they need something, they'll call. They've been told. *Warned.*

I head to the kitchen, where Jasper's money still sits on the table. I dump the wash bucket down the kitchen sink. The water is a mixture of pinkish brown, from the dust and blood in the carpet. It reminds me that I should vacuum more, but I already know I won't. Then I set the empty bucket aside and sigh wearily.

I was counting on not having any guests tonight. It surprises me that anyone would show up in weather like this, let alone this many people. Granted, two of them are only here looking for the first. How is he doing, anyway?

I return down the hall and back to the stairs, but I only manage to climb halfway before someone tries to open the door behind me. The doorknob jiggles, but of course it's locked.

Go away, I think.

What else could they possibly need? Isn't it late enough as it is? Why aren't they all in bed yet?

Whoever's out there begins to knock. *Aggressively.* They pound like it's an emergency. Maybe it is. With yet another weary sigh, I start down the stairs again. I pause just on the other side of the door. It's an effort to muster what little cordiality remains inside me. My skills in hospitality are failing me tonight. I just don't have the energy I used to…

The knocking continues, a single, meaty fist thumping the door to command my attention, and I grit my teeth in response. I unlock the deadbolt and open the door just a crack, as though I'm indecent. It's not the young woman this time, but the *other* one. The man. He checked in under *Jason,* but I know that's probably not his real name, not if he's any association of Jasper's.

"Oh," I say. "Is there something I can do for you, sir?"

He's mostly dark, standing with his back to the red light of our sign, but I can see his face well enough to recognize the hardened impatience on his brow, as the snow continues to swirl and billow behind him.

"Where is he?" Jason says.

My blood runs cold in an instant. I do my best to control my face, to appear confused and not give myself away.

"I'm sorry?"

"I know he's in there somewhere." He steps closer, his face between the gap, and I place the toe of my boot against this side of the door, just in case. "Is he dead or alive?"

I scoff—a most convincing display of offense.

"Sir, what on earth are you talking about?"

"Maybe he's not going by Jasper. Maybe he gave you

another name. But I know he's here, and I know *you know* exactly who I'm talking about."

"I have no idea—"

"That truck out there? That's *mine*. He stole it from me. Now it's here. And judging by the blood I just found in his room, I think I can safely guess what you were scrubbing out of the carpet when we first arrived. Am I wrong?"

My blood is ice. My stomach plummets like I'm in free fall. I can feel my own pulse ticking through my throat. For a moment, I'm speechless.

"So I ask you again," he says. "Where is he?"

I struggle to find words in order to keep this lie going.

"I really don't know what you're talking about. But unless there's something else you need, I'm locking up for the—"

My boot against the door doesn't do me any good as he shoulders into it, throwing the door wide open with all his brute strength. It hits me hard and sends me spinning, falling. I barely catch myself with my fingers in the carpet. I push myself upright, pivoting on my heel as I retreat backward, until I bump against the front counter. The man called Jason steps into my home, throws the door shut behind him.

He reaches into his jacket and pulls out a gun.

"Enough with the games. Tell me where he is, or this gets a whole lot uglier."

I put my empty hands into the air in a display of submission. I'm flustered, to say the least.

"The man you're looking for... he..." My thoughts are racing. My heart is racing. "He was injured when he arrived. He was *gravely* injured. He'd already lost a lot of blood, and…"

"Where is he?" Jason repeats, taking another step closer.

"I tried to help him, but… he's dead. He died."

Jason doesn't flinch as I say this, but I can see the shift in his eyes.

"And did you call the police?"

"Yes." My voice cracks a little, scratchy with nerves. "I did."

His eyes narrow. A few seconds pass but feel like minutes. I don't think he believes me.

"What did you do with the money?"

"Money?"

"Yes, the money. It's not in his room, and I know he wouldn't have left it in the truck. Where did you put it?"

I can't continue lying. I mean, I *could*, but it won't do me any good at this point. He sees through me. If I don't start going along with him, things will only get messier. Or *uglier*, as he put it.

"Here. Follow me…"

I turn into the hallway. He follows close. I can practically feel his eyes burning a hole in the back of my head, and the barrel of his gun burning a hole in my back. I need to do whatever I can to keep that hole a metaphorical one.

I take him to the kitchen table where the duffel bag sits. As he sees the bag, he gives me a violent shove, forcing me to stumble toward the kitchen counter where I barely catch myself. I lean there a moment, my breaths shallow, my legs trembling. Behind me, he begins examining the money. I listen as he opens the bag and his hand shuffles around inside for a moment. With my head bent, I lift my gaze to the counter before me, to the cutlery block there that holds all my largest kitchen knives.

"Where's the rest of it?" he says.

I turn slightly, my chin against my shoulder. "Huh?"

"There's money missing. A lot of it, actually. Where'd you stash it?"

"I didn't touch your money."

He grabs the bag and tips it toward me, holding it open so that I can see what's left inside. I think he might be right. There does appear to be less money in there now than I remember. Enough to notice even at just a glance. I open my mouth to answer but can't find the words. I shrug helplessly instead.

"I didn't touch any of it, I swear—"

There comes a loud *thump* above us, directly over our heads. We each freeze, before lifting our gazes to the ceiling in unison. I return my attention to Jason. He returns his attention to me. A moment of silence. A moment of mutual understanding.

"Huh," he says, looking me in the eye. "Dead, you say?"

Without another word he starts down the hallway, legs swishing in haste. I look about myself, temporarily stunned, deciding what I might do to stop him.

JASPER

I'm hot and scratchy when I wake. Sweaty. For a few seconds my vision is soft and uncentered. The lamp is on. I blink sleep from my eyes. I'm still too heavy to move, too exhausted, but I'm able to lift my head slightly from my pillow, looking down at myself where I lay. I've been dressed in someone's sweater. A rough, green, wool sweater. As I study it, and myself, I catch a potent whiff of cologne. It almost makes me sneeze.

The bedroom door is closed and I'm alone.

I lay my head back into my pillow. I breathe deeply, catching repeated traces of that cologne smell, like it's been sprayed on me directly. I don't know the scent. It's not mine, obviously. I've never worn cologne in my life... even though Jennifer has hinted before that she likes it.

Jennifer.

I'm not safe. I need to get out of here as soon as possible, although it doesn't feel at all possible right now. I curl my fingers into fists. I wiggle my toes. I go so far as pulling one leg toward myself, my knee rising beneath the covers. I *can* move, but I'm sluggish. It won't be enough to overcome…

Her. What is her name?

I don't know her name. I don't know anything about her, except that she runs this motel and she's… insane?

Dangerous.

I try to sit up, lifting my head again. My skull aches. My muscles ache. My parched lips are close to cracking. It's like the worst hangover of my life. The tray of food is still sitting on the nightstand. Cold soup. *Drugged* soup. I don't know how it's possible that I escaped Erik's thugs and somehow managed to end up someplace entirely worse. Yes, this is worse. At least when it comes to Quentin and the others I know what I'm up against. They're just following orders, looking to score some points with the boss. I don't know what this woman wants from me, or why. Whatever her plans are, I'm not meant to leave this place. I know that somehow. The fear inside me is a deep one, an instinct I'm not sure I've ever tapped into before.

Jennifer once told me what it can be like to date as a woman—the constant, subliminal uncertainty of your own safety. I suppose the danger I'm in now is a helluva lot more than *subliminal,* but still. It's different than any kind of danger I've been in before. Unpredictable. Unknowable.

Does she intend to hurt me?

I remind myself that she's patched up my wounds. That should imply that she means to *help* me, not harm me. But I can't shake the feeling. The danger. For fuck's sake, I woke up with her tongue in my mouth, and now…

Now?

Whose sweater is this? Whose cologne?

With immense effort, I push myself up onto my elbows. It's enough to make me want to roll over and go back to sleep. A hellish hangover and the flu wrapped into one. I can't even sit straight, or stiffen my shoulders. They're slack and lazy and so damn heavy. I can barely hold my head upright. It's a monumental effort to swivel my legs off the edge of the bed, to place my feet onto the floor, but I manage it. Somehow I manage it. It makes it easier for me to hunch there with my hands on my knees, my head bent. I breathe deeply. Even now I'm tempted to simply plop back onto the bed and fall asleep with my leg's dangling off its edge. There's a subtle, throbbing pain in my gut. The gunshot. I'm still wounded, of course. Tender.

I'm given pause once again as I remind myself that she patched up my wounds.

Perhaps if I stay and… and…

And what? Play along? If I stay and play along, she'll let me go once I'm better? She did mention something about taking me to the hospital in the morning, if the storm has cleared enough.

Why don't I believe her?

Because she's drugged you.

She said it was to help me sleep. Was that true? Or was it so she could climb on top of me while I did?

Does it even really matter so long as she keeps her word about the hospital?

I don't think I want to find out. My gut—my bullet-torn gut—is telling me I need to get out of this place.

I sit forward, putting most of my weight onto my feet. I place my hand on the edge of the nightstand for support.

My legs tremble, actually *tremble,* as I try to stand. What is happening to me? Maybe it's a combination of the drugs *and* the injuries, the blood loss, all of it. At least my mind is more alert than it was. And the more I exert myself, the clearer my thoughts seem to become as I pry myself from sleep's clutches.

Where do you think you're going to go?

Maybe I'm not thinking nearly as clearly as I thought. But it doesn't matter. I can't sit and wait for things to get worse—however they might.

I put all my strength into standing, lifting myself off the bed, simultaneously leaning against the nightstand for support until I stumble against it. My hand slides across its surface to catch myself and I knock the lamp over in the process. It topples sideways and hits the carpet with a soft but heavy thud. I barely keep standing with both hands on the nightstand now, panting, out of breath and energy both.

Nice job, numb nuts.

Oh well. I press on. Slowly. I let go of the nightstand entirely, trusting my legs to hold me steady on their own. I wobble a bit, but I'm standing. I drag my feet two whole steps from the nightstand toward the door across the room, and suddenly I feel as though I'm swimming—that sensation that washes over you when you don't realize how drunk you really are until you're standing. My trembling legs threaten to give out. I step toward the bed beside me, leaning against it before I collapse. I fall to my knees, catch myself against the side of the bed, awkwardly slumped against it.

That's when I hear them coming.

Footsteps approach outside. Heavy boots. Deliberate. Stomping. They're not her footsteps. Someone else's.

Sagging against the side of the bed, I look toward the bedroom door as the footsteps arrive outside, where they stop and linger, listening.

"Jasper? You in here, buddy?"

It's him. It's Quentin. Somehow he's found me. Somehow he knows I'm up here. But how? The craziest part is that I'm not entirely disappointed. There's a part of me that's *glad* to hear his voice, as if there's any chance he's come to save me from this strange nightmare and not just to end it entirely.

The door opens. He steps through. He's already got his gun in his hand. This isn't a rescue mission. He's come to finish what he started. Only my delirious mind could have hoped otherwise. Except, as he enters the room and his eyes dart about for an instant before centering on me, he appears shocked to see me as I am—on the floor, clinging to the edge of the bed in my underwear and someone's sweater. I imagine I look like I'm half dead already. I know I did when I saw myself in the bathroom mirror of my motel room.

"What the…" Quentin starts to say but trails off.

He shakes his head, ridding himself of his confusion. He takes one step into the room, aims his gun directly at me, and stops again. His eyes grow wide. His mouth opens in a strange and terrible gasp, lips pulling back from his teeth. He lowers his gun as each of his arms seem to straighten out on either side of him, as he lifts onto the toes of his boots. It's only then I notice the second pair of legs behind him.

His eyes dart to their corners in acknowledgement of his

attacker, before he promptly crumples to the floor. He lands hard, his head thumping off the carpet. The woman stands over him. She's visibly shaking from head to toe, huffing and puffing as her gaze wanders to me, then back to Quentin and the knife handle still sticking out of his lower spine.

LANA

*M*y grandma is sitting up against the headboard when I return inside, with my grandpa's urn in her lap. She smiles as I enter. I lock the door behind me.

"Now who's picking at scabs?" I say.

The smile on her face contorts with offense. "This isn't picking at scabs…"

"When you really think about it, isn't this entire trip just one big scab we're picking?"

"This trip is to honor your grandfather's wishes, Lana. This is *not* picking at scabs or anything of the sort…"

"I'm joking, Grandma."

"Well… I'm not laughing."

Now I give her a look. It's not unlike the look she gives me when I'm being ridiculous. She lowers her gaze to the shiny urn in her lap, however, pretending I'm not giving her any look at all.

"Although," I go on, "given the amount of times I've heard you complain about him over the years…"

"Well, of course I've complained about him. He was a man, after all." She sighs pleasantly, like she's reminiscing. "He could be a real asshole sometimes. But mostly he was just clueless. So many of them are. But he was *my* clueless asshole, and I loved him dearly…"

"You're not setting the bar very high."

"Oh, women are assholes, too, Lana. And plenty clueless."

"Hmm," I say, "I might agree with the first part, but I don't think *I'm* clueless."

I start taking off my coat until I remember all the cash stuffed in my pockets. I walk to the other side of my bed and carefully drop to my knees next to my luggage bag so that what I'm doing isn't visible to her.

"Oh, we're *all* clueless, dear. Every last one of us. Men and women. You're no exception. I think you know that. We're all assholes, too, in our own selfish ways…"

"Wow, Grandma, I had no idea you were such a pessimist…"

I'm distracted as I say this, as I begin pulling out those bound wads of cash again. My stomach tightens at the sight of them. I slip them into my bag, underneath my folded clothes.

"It's not pessimism. It's just the way it is. We're born knowing nothing, we die long before we figure much out…" I glance up from my nefarious business to see her turning my grandpa's urn, studying its every inch. "…and at the end of the day, we're nothing more than a bunch of needy, self-interested animals. We spend most of our lives thinking of ourselves. And *gosh,* do we take so much for granted. It seems it's only ever at the last possible minute that we realize what we have… or had."

I finish tucking all of the money away. I stand up, then plop onto the edge of my bed and begin taking off my boots. I have nothing to add to my grandma's philosophizing, so I change the subject.

"The motel manager was watching that movie you love so much, by the way. I can't remember what it's called. It's got that guy in it from *Schindler's List*. What's his name? You have a crush on him, I think."

"Liam Neeson?"

"No, the other one. I think he plays the bad guy."

"Oh, Ralph Fiennes?" she says, and the way she says it makes me cock my head toward my shoulder, my eyes narrowed skeptically. *RAYF Fines.*

"Is that really how you say it?" I ask, then shrug indifferently. My grandma would know better than anyone. "Anyway, yeah, him. It's the one where he's in the desert. I think he ends up in the hospital or something…"

"Oh, *The English Patient!*" my grandma exclaims excitedly. "Oh, I *do* love that movie…"

I slide my last boot off my foot and onto the floor, then stand straight again, hands on my hips.

"You've just got the hots for Ralph Fiennes."

"Yes, and?" she says, not even denying it. "Am I wrong?"

I collect some things from my bag—my toothbrush and toothpaste and my face wash and moisturizer—and take them to the bathroom, now that it's finally my turn to get ready for bed. I shut the door behind me. I meet my own gaze in the mirror as I begin brushing my teeth, under the bright, ugly overhead light, and my grandma's words repeat like an echo in my mind.

...we're nothing more than a bunch of needy, self-interested animals...

She's probably right about that. She's right about a lot of things, actually, though I'll never admit that to her face.

I spit into the sink and watch the foamy toothpaste swirl around the drain.

I just hope she isn't right about me, is all.

MISSY

*T*he past minute or so is just a blur. Last I recall, I was standing in the kitchen against the counter while I watched the man called Jason storm through my house and out of sight. Now I'm upstairs, and Jason is on the floor. Jasper is on the floor as well, clutching the bed how a toddler clutches their mother's leg. The lamp is on the floor. I feel something wet on my index finger, where my hand had momentarily been pressed to Jason's back, where the blade of the knife had embedded itself into his spine...

Embedded itself?

I've never done anything like this before. I don't have the stomach for physical violence. Even now my stomach lurches inside me. I feel my bile churning, growing hot. I take deep, heavy breaths to soothe it, to stop it from rising into my throat. I don't want to vomit. I've enough to clean up as it is.

But I can't take my eyes off of him. The dead man. The protruding knife. Did I really do that? I guess I did. The longer I stand in shock, the clearer the last minute becomes in my memory. The blur of it all sharpens, so that I remember pulling the knife from the cutlery block, and my brief journey down the hallway, up the stairs, chasing after Jason before he learned…

Learned…

Before he learned that Jasper is still alive, of course. That I'm caring for him. That I'm protecting him.

I'm shocked that I had it in me. I hardly even considered the action. There was no time for consideration. I did what I *had* to. I did what needed to be done in order to save Jasper's life.

I regard him now, still slumped against the bed, looking at me with those pitiful eyes of his. There's a feverishness about him. His gaze is *loose*, meandering. For the brief moments he looks at me, his fear is palpable. He doesn't understand.

"You… you…" He struggles to speak. His mouth is as loose as his gaze. "You killed him…"

I look to the dead man at my feet.

"I was only protecting you, Geoffrey. He came looking for you, and—"

"Jasper," he says, and the fear upon his brow is transformed to utter disgust. Horror. Like I'm some kind of monster. He's confused, obviously.

Admittedly, I'm a little confused, too. A slip of the tongue. My mind is reeling in so many directions.

"Oh, right. Of course. I'm sorry." My cheeks burn hot with embarrassment. I move past Jasper and set the lamp back on the nightstand. I quickly peer through the window blinds into the dark, but it's difficult to see anything. I turn to Jasper once again. "Here… let's get you back into bed, before you hurt yourself."

Using the bed, Jasper pulls himself away, as if he stands any chance of resisting me in his sorry state.

"Don't touch me," he says.

He's talking crazy, clearly. I crouch over him, try to scoop my hands beneath his armpits to help him up. He shrugs away from me, releasing his grasp on the bedcovers and falling to the floor upon his back. I have to step over him now, practically straddling him in order to hook my hands under his arms and—

"Don't touch me!" he shouts.

He rolls in my arms and I drop him flat on his chest. He's obviously not as tired as he *should* be. A bubble of anger rises in me. I can't stop it from bursting open, scalding hot from my tongue.

"Damn you!" I say. I'm overcome with the urge to kick him, but I resist. Barely. "I'm trying to *help you,* for God's sake…"

I bend over him once more. I scoop him up from behind this time. His arms flail about like a child's, weak and imprecise. I struggle to lift him as his weight shifts in my grasp, as he fights to roll out from under me again.

"Stop it," I growl, my teeth clenched. The sound of my voice is hardly flattering, hardly endearing.

"You… drugged me," he says, still flopping about like a giant fish.

"It was for your own good. You need to rest. You need to *heal,* Jasper. You're not going to survive your wounds if you don't rest and let them *heal…*"

I'm honestly baffled that he's got this much fight in him. I'm baffled that he's even awake.

As it becomes increasingly clear that I'll be unable to hoist him back into bed, I drop him for the second time. He rolls himself onto his back, his arms raised to fight me off. But I don't come for him again. Not yet. I stomp around him, to the nightstand and the tray of food there. I grab the half-eaten bowl of soup. It's cold by now, but it doesn't matter. This isn't for his enjoyment.

"You're leaving me no choice," I tell him. I hunch over him again, the bowl in one hand, the spoon in the other. "Now open up."

I drop to my knees beside him. He turns away from me. Thinking quickly, I discard the spoon altogether. I'll need a spare hand to hold him still, to pry him open.

"Come on, Jasper," I say. "Open your mouth."

I grab him by the face and turn him toward me. He grasps me by the arm, but he's not strong enough to pull my hand away. I pinch his mouth between my fingers, feeling his teeth through the flesh of his cheeks. I manage to grab him by his jaw, which I pull open, his mouth yawning wide as I tip the entire bowl of soup toward him. It spills out, a clean rivulet of yellow broth. First it pours over his chin before it splashes into his open mouth. He fights me still, trying to turn away. Without much thought, I put my knee upon his stomach to pin him in place, forgetting all about his bandages, the wound underneath. He screams in pain, his mouth yawning wider, opening up for the soup I'm still pouring into his gaping maw.

"That's it. That's it—"

He coughs, splutters, spitting a fine mist of broth into

the air, onto *me*. His mouth and my hand become slippery with soup, enough that he's finally able to jerk his face out of my grasp. The bowl slips out of my hand similarly, spilling what soup is left all over him, all over the sweater I've dressed him in. *Your* sweater.

Another bubble rises in me. A bubble of rage.

"Look what you've done!" My voice is shrill and crazed. I can't help it. I squeeze my hands into fists. "Don't make me into the bad guy here, Jasper. I'm *not* the bad guy..."

The bowl is now empty, the soup spilled mostly everywhere but down his throat. I set it aside. Running out of patience, I grab hold of him again and heave him upright. Strengthened by my own temper, I lift him against the side of the bed, onto the bed, where I shove him down, grab him by the legs, and swing them onto the mattress likewise. I jerk the covers out from under him, sweep them over him once more. Then I drag him back into place, where he should have been laying all along, and shove his pillow under his head while he continues to cough and choke.

"Oh, just *stop it* already," I tell him, as his wheezing inches toward theatrics at this point. "You did this to yourself."

I pull the covers up over his soup-dampened chest. He simply lies there, coughing gently. He turns his head away from me like a petulant toddler. He appears too exhausted to carry on now, at least. That's fine by me. I've got so much work to do.

Jason's on the floor exactly as I left him. His gun lies just beside his limp hand. I quickly snatch it up. I study it for a moment, dangling delicately between my pinched fingers as though it could go off at the slightest touch. I should get rid of it, too, I think, before it somehow finds itself into the wrong pair of hands. There's a red indicator near the gun's trigger, which I believe means it's ready to shoot. I flip the switch, hiding the red dot. Then I tuck the gun into the back of my waistband for the time being. I'll find a better place for it soon.

Next I crouch next to Jason's body, eyeing the knife handle sticking out of his back. It bears repeating—I don't like physical violence. I'm hesitant to even pull the knife free. Instead I reach into his various pockets until I find his wallet. He's got a good bit of cash inside. I examine his driver's license and discover that his real name is Quentin Andrews. I figured as much. He doesn't look like a Jason. Somehow he *does* look like a Quentin.

I take his wallet into my bedroom and toss it into the bottom drawer of my nightstand. Then I pull his pistol from my waistband. Should I throw this one in the trash downstairs as well? As much as I *loathe* the thought, I might need it. Quentin's partner is still out there and will be wondering where he went before long. Things could get out of hand— more so than they already have. I tuck the gun back into my waistband and return to the guest bedroom. Jasper hasn't moved, his head still turned away like it was. Has he fallen asleep again? I think he's just given up. Either possibility is fine by me.

I grab Quentin by the feet and proceed to drag him from the guest room and into the hall, to the head of the stairs. The knife handle quivers in his spine as we go. I drag him down the stairs rather carelessly. Luckily he's on his stomach, and I don't think he's leaked enough blood yet to be making a mess on my carpet from that side. He thumps rather sickeningly down each step, his head and hands rumbling along in quick succession. I drag him from the bottom of the stairs directly to the front door. There, I grab my heavy coat from the rack in the corner. I slip into it, zip it up all the way up underneath my chin. I take the gun from my waistband and stuff it into my coat pocket where it's much more comfortable.

Erring on the side of caution, I pull my hood onto my head and step outside into the storm to survey the road and the parking lot, ensuring that nobody's coming from any direction. I walk around the corner of the house and peer toward Room 16 at the back of the lot, confirming neither of the women are coming to bother me again at this particular moment.

I should have enough time, I think.

I return inside, grab Quentin by his ankles, and haul him across the threshold, onto the snowy walkway. I drag him away from our home, away from the motel, toward the bordering fields. His body leaves an indented trail in the snow, but it'll be covered again in no time. I'm not worried.

I drag him into the snow-flattened weeds beyond our property, to a spot I know is safe. I won't be able to dig any time soon. The ground is too cold, too hard. But the snow will bury him soon enough, and he can stay that way for a good long while without being noticed.

I let go of him. His limp arms are outstretched, as if he's reaching for our motel. I trace the path his body's made in the snow with my eyes, peering toward our house, dark and cold with just the faintest glow of red light along the edge of its silhouette where our sign stands out front. I sigh heavily. My vision clouds with my own breath. I regard the dead man at my feet and wonder how long it'll be before his partner becomes a problem, too. I should probably deal with him sooner rather than later.

I crouch beside Quentin's corpse. I bite down as I grab the handle of the knife, willing my stomach to stay settled. I pull the knife free with a single tug. It comes easily enough, a tassel of bright red blood trailing from its tip. I'm reminded of snow cone syrup. My gurgling stomach doesn't much like the comparison.

Hold it together, Missy.

I hear these words in your voice. It's comforting.

I take the knife back with me, across the field and back to the house. I stomp my boots on the mat outside before stepping into the lovely warmth of the front room. I lock the door behind me. I take the knife into the kitchen and rinse it under the faucet. The pink water swirls around the white ceramic, down the black hole of the drain. Then, as I pull the knife out from under the water, I catch my reflection on its surface.

My gaze is more relaxed than I'd expect.

I go to the table, where the bag of money is still pulled wide open from Quentin's hands previously. I take another look myself, confirming once more that he was right—there's money missing. I'm certain of it. But who could have taken it? Besides Jasper, there have only been two people inside my home tonight—Quentin and the woman from Room 16. Quentin obviously wouldn't have taken his own money and then been surprised by it.

So that leaves the woman.

She'd come asking for more blankets. I'd fallen asleep upstairs. For how long had I slept? Was it long enough that she'd had free reign of our house? Long enough for her to snoop through our kitchen? Through this bag of money? Obviously she'd done exactly that. It's the only explanation I can think of. Is she really so stupid to think her theft would go unnoticed? But also...

Do I even care?

It was never my money to begin with. There's still a lot of it left in the bag. I'd be smart not to blow things out of proportion, I think. I don't need her attention on me. Tonight is a mess enough as it is, and I've still got Quentin's companion to deal with. I need to nip that problem in the bud. Quentin had a gun. His partner likely has one as well. For now, I still have the element of surprise on my side.

I realize I'm still holding the rinsed kitchen knife—gripping it tight enough to whiten my knuckles.

How does the saying go?

Desperate times call for desperate measures?

ALLEN

*W*hat a fucked up deal this whole night has become. I should have known we were in for a sloppy mess when Quentin first told me to *take some cheap shots* from the passenger seat of the truck. Erik never would have given us orders like that. Erik prefers to keep things subtle, unnoticed. Everything we've done tonight has been brazen.

I don't even want to think about what Quentin's getting up to now, dealing with the motel manager whom he seems to think has answers to everything we're looking for. We're in deep shit no matter what. We made a mess of Jasper's car and left it out there for anybody to find. We left Wyatt's body out there for anybody to find. Sure, the blizzard will probably hide it for a bit. Maybe enough time for us to clean up before anyone's the wiser, I don't know.

I just don't know.

In a way, I'm glad I took a bullet to the leg. It gives me an excuse to lay back, hang low, and let Quentin clean up his own mess. Because this is *his* mess, I think. Yeah, I made the mistake of listening to him, but that's quite literally my job tonight. I'm following orders. Quentin was put in charge of this wild goose chase. Erik called him, not me. I'm simply the tagalong.

Whatever he's doing in the manager's house right now, he better get things sorted, and quick.

My leg hurts like hell. It's a *deep* ache all through my shin. The bullet struck bone, splintered into God knows how many directions. It's too painful to stand on for long, which is why I've resigned myself to lying in bed until Quentin comes back.

I don't know what's taking him so long.

If he's right about the motel manager harboring Jasper in some capacity, it should be fairly simple to learn. Intimidation is our bread and butter. Take back the money, the keys to the truck, and we can be on our way, easy peasy...

I'm tempted to peer out the window, but even shifting around too much where I lay on the bedcovers sends shooting pain through my leg, all the way up into my kneecap.

Shooting pain, ha!

Hopefully Quentin will return soon and we can get the hell out of here.

I close my eyes, take a deep breath. Then another.

And another.

I've already dozed off many times tonight, but it's not my fault. I'm an *'in bed by eight o clock'* kinda guy. It's already so late, and that's not even accounting for how exhausting this night has been.

Quentin's handling it. He'll be back soon. With the money. With the keys. Then we can go.

We'll be on the road again in no time. I'll be home in no time. I'll be in bed in no time...

I'm starting to drift off again when the door opens. I barely stir. Even my eyes are too heavy at this point to bother looking as Quentin comes in, shutting the door quietly behind him.

That's polite of him, I think.

"It's about time," I murmur, my lips as lazy as my eyes. "I was... starting to worry you'd—"

An incredibly strange sensation crosses me. Across my throat. I open my eyes then, as it comes—warm, tingling, *sharp.* It's not Quentin I see standing over me. A face I don't recognize. A woman. A beautiful woman I've never seen before. That strange sensation stiffens me as my mind makes sense of it, as it becomes clearer. It's a new kind of pain. I've been hurt. I feel the hot aftermath trickling around either side of me, to the back of my neck, my head sunken into the pillow. My immediate reflex is to clap a hand to the sensation, my body understanding what's happened before my mind does, apparently. And then I feel it, my own opened flesh against the palm of my hand. Wet and pulsing. My mouth yawns but I can't speak. I can't scream. I can't even gasp. All that escapes me is a pitiful gurgle.

The woman holds a knife. Its edge is wet with my blood.

My mind kicks into gear with its next reflex.

Get away.

I attempt to roll off the bed, but she scrambles on top of me in an instant. She forces me down, forces me to stay exactly as I am, on my back with my blood still pumping out of me.

"Let's not make an even bigger mess now," she says through her teeth, her hands on either of my shoulders to keep me in place. "I've scrubbed enough carpet tonight."

With my life draining out of me, what little light is in the room seems to drain away similarly. Everything grows dark. Faded. Her beautiful face—twisted scornfully into something else—fades away with the rest of it, as the darkness closes in around me. As sleep closes in.

I doze off for one last time.

MISSY

There's an unexpected kindness in his eyes as the light leaves them. Maybe there'd always been a kindness in them, but his fear of me, of his *situation*, had previously masked it. I feel sorry for him. For a moment or two. But I truly had no choice in this matter. He and his partner have left me no choice.

Much of his blood has gotten on the bed, but that's all right. Bedsheets can be replaced. That's why I chose the knife over the gun. Less mess. It's also quieter. The very *last* thing I need is to accidentally draw the attention of the other guests with gunfire.

All things considered, this went much smoother than I could have hoped. I was lucky to catch him unaware.

I carefully crawl off of him, off the bed, standing by his side with the knife still in my hand. Once again it's dirtied with blood. I take it into the bathroom where the light is already on. I drop it into the bathroom sink and leave it there for a short while as I just stand and study myself in the bathroom mirror. I'm tired. I look it. I've also got blood on my face. It's smeared, like someone's wiped their bloody hand across my cheek. Had he done that? I hadn't noticed in the moment. A squeamish chill runs up my body. I turn on the water and rinse my hands, then frantically rinse the blood from off my face.

They hit me all at once—too many emotions and feelings to sort through. Everything blurs as my eyes fill with tears. I finish washing my face, turn off the water, and dry myself on the bathroom towel. I pat my leaky eyes dry on the bathroom towel as well. I take a deep breath.

Control yourself.

I leave the knife in the sink the way it is. I stand in the bathroom doorway, lean there as I study the gruesome scene I've made. Another body. Another bloody mess.

My stomach lurches. Hot bile rises up the back of my throat. I feel it coming. *Taste it* coming. I turn and crash onto my knees as I fling open the toilet lid and retch. It's awful. This feeling. The sounds I'm making. I retch until I'm empty inside. Then I stand on wobbly legs. I run the faucet again, sip some cool water, rinse my mouth out and spit. Then I return to the bathroom doorway and test my luck a second time, studying my horrendous work.

I don't have the energy to drag him anywhere, let alone across the entire parking lot and into the field next to his buddy. That's a long way to drag a body, and I've already dragged two tonight.

I wish you were here. If you were still here, none of this would have happened. Life in general would be so different now if you were still around. So, so different. I can't even imagine it, though I often try.

Why did you do it?

Why did you have to hurt me?

Why did you betray me?

"Why are you all so disappointing..." I mumble as I peer across the dimly lit room at yet another dead man whose mess I have to clean up.

I'm not cleaning this up tonight. That's already decided. Before I leave, however, I take a look through the dead man's pockets until I find his wallet. I investigate his driver's license, where I learn his name was Allen Sommers.

Allen. Quentin. Jasper.

Criminals and liars, all of them.

Jasper, you stupid, handsome fool...

In my sensitive state, my mind wanders to places it shouldn't. I'm reminded of those pictures on his phone—of the naked woman, of *him*—and my body burns with an entanglement of excitement and jealousy. He reminds me of you in so many ways. Too many ways. The best ways *and* the worst ways...

It's too late at night and I'm too overwhelmed to filter these thoughts and feelings brewing inside me. It's a perfect storm, as perfectly bitter and cold as the storm still raging outside, and suddenly I'm brimming with it again. An anger I can't quell. Before I even realize what I'm doing, where I'm headed, I'm hastily stomping my way outside, moving swiftly through the snow, back to the house. *Our* house. I step into the lobby, throw the door shut behind me, and stride quickly up the stairs.

This is all his fault.

It's true. Everything's gone to hell since he showed up,

bringing all his troubles to my doorstep. All I've done is try to help him, and for what? More troublesome men, more bodies to bury.

And to think he's still wearing your sweater, tainting it with his *foulness...*

Everything blurs again, but not with tears. I storm into the guest bedroom where he still lies in a pathetic heap. I arrive at his bedside, out of breath and trembling. His eyes are open. He looks at me, his gaze bright and glistening with... what is that? Fear?

"Why did you come here?" I say, my voice splitting, on edge.

My hand lashes out before I can stop myself. A rattlesnake. A whip crack. His face turns sidewards, his cheek hot and chafed by the swipe of my palm. I slap him again. And again. And again. He utters not a sound. I don't know that he can. But that pathetic, wide-eyed face of his recoils with each strike. I grab hold of him, my thumb curved along the hard line of his jaw, my fingernails dimpling the flesh of his cheek.

"How could you do this to me?"

I take my hand away rough and fast, my fingernails raking him along the way, and by then my eyes are full of tears. His visage swims in my vision. Impossibly, *painfully* familiar.

"You... you *worthless...*" I grab two fistfuls of the wool sweater and begin pulling it up along his torso, revealing his bare chest. *"Worthless!"*

I pull the sweater from off his head and arms in a single tug, leaving him to flop back into place like the invalid he is. I stomp out of the room, your sweater balled up in my hand. I take it into our bedroom, to our bed, where I collapse in a pathetic pile of my own, your sweater pressed against my hot, tear-streaked cheek, and I begin to sob.

QUENTIN

*M*y eyes are frosted shut. My fingers are chilled to the bone. My skull aches where I thumped my head on the floor and my back aches where I've been stabbed.

I can't feel my legs at all.

I pry open my eyes and all I see is white. So much cold white. I close my fingers around it, the white, and my frozen knuckles crack with the effort, brittle as ice. I inhale the cold into my lungs and wheeze. Each cough sends my body vibrating in the snow, sends the wound in my back sparking with agony. That wound reaches deep, deeper than just my back, into the meat of me. Vital things have been struck.

I am not in good shape.

I can't decide if I'm lucky or unlucky. Am I lucky that she believed I was dead? Am I lucky that I'm *not* dead? Or would I be better off without a pulse at this point?

I will myself to stand but my legs don't respond. Not one bit. Nothing below my waist has any sensation that I can feel at the moment. It happened when she first plunged her knife into my lower back. Into my spine. She severed me there. I'd gone down like a felled tree and rocked my head pretty good in the fall. And before any of that had happened, I'd seen him.

Jasper is alive. She's protecting him.

I suppose he doesn't matter right now. I suppose the money doesn't even matter right now. The only thing that matters is that I survive this. I'm not feeling too optimistic about my chances, but I still need to try.

I've still got some strength in my upper body. I lift my head out of the snow and blink my snow-crusted eyes. The motel isn't far. I see it's dark shape framed against a half-border of red light, where the roadside sign silhouettes it on the other side. I see the parking lot behind the manager's home, where the lamppost flickers off and on and off and on, the snow still eddying down in its light. The snow is indeed still coming down, and if I don't do something soon I'll be buried.

So I reach. I grab the snow, both old and new. My fingers sink through the fresh powdery stuff and into the crunchy old stuff, crunchy enough to bite me back. I drag myself, little by little. My hands are already numb. My fingertips twinge with it. I continue reaching, grabbing, pulling. I'm moving. That's all that matters. I don't know how long it takes me, but the parking lot comes closer and closer with each pull. The dark sky above sheds its ice onto me the whole way. My legs drag uselessly behind me. And here I'd thought Allen was useless with his *one* injured leg.

I wonder what he's up to now.

It isn't too long before I reach the edge of the field I've

been dumped in. Even though I continue pulling myself across snow, I notice the change between the weedy dirt and the parking lot's asphalt. It's harder underneath my body, firmer. My hands are not only completely numb by this point, but they're bleeding, thoroughly chewed by the ragged ice. My arms are sore, my shoulders screaming. I approach the blinking lamppost's cone of intermittent light. Best to avoid it, I think. I take the easier way around, the closer route, which happens to follow along the motel itself, away from the woman's home, away from my truck still parked behind it. I pull myself along the motel's slightly covered walkway. The snow hasn't built up as much there, out of the wind's trajectory. I drag myself through it, my numb fingers greedy for anything not covered in ice.

I have to stop for a moment. I'm panting, out of breath, my lungs simultaneously on fire and aching from the cold air. I don't believe I have the strength to drag myself back to my own room. Back to Allen. Not to mention, my room is under the brighter lamppost. At the rate I'm dragging myself, I wouldn't be surprised to be so unlucky that the manager happens to peer outside while I'm exposed under that light. I'm much closer to *their* room. The women. The young bitch and the old bitch.

Am I desperate enough for that?

Apparently I am, because after few minutes of rest I continue dragging myself there.

LANA

*M*y little smoke break calmed me some, but as soon as I climb under the covers with the lights off, my mind is restless again. My whole body is restless. I toss and turn while my grandma lies perfectly still like a mummy in a sarcophagus. I think she's already asleep.

I can't stop thinking about the money. I'm giddy with excitement, nervous with doubt, as well as eaten up with guilt. It's a weird combination, I know. I'm excited by the prospect of getting away with it. I'm nervous about getting caught. I'm guilty for having taken it at all. Obviously I don't feel *that* guilty, or else I wouldn't have taken it in the first place, right? Mostly I feel guilty because I know my actions could have severe consequences. Not just for myself, but for my grandma as well. This trip is special to her. I genuinely don't want to ruin it. That's the last thing I want.

You should really get a handle on these bad habits of yours…
These things don't serve you, Lana…

Between my bouts of flopping under the covers, laying with my face half-buried into my pillow, I hear a noise that snaps my eyes wide open—rodent feet clawing in the far corners of the room, scurrying along the baseboards. I peer into the darkness, listening. My heart immediately begins to race. If there's an actual rat in our room, snooping through our bags, or worse, climbing into bed with us, sniffing around our feet... The mere thought makes me pull my legs inward, curling up into a fetal position.

The clawing sounds continue. I sit up slightly, propped on my elbow.

Scratch, scratch, scratch.

It must be rats. Disgusting. Or mice. Some kind of vermin, anyway. The specifics aren't important. I was already struggling to relax. There's no way I'm sleeping after this.

Then, as I sit and listen with my every muscle tensed in revulsion, the sound changes. The scratching becomes knocking. Soft and rhythmic. Deliberate, almost. I'm not sure what to make of it. Could a rat make a noise like that? I turn to see my grandma across the chasm of darkness between our beds, her bed closer to the bathroom, mine closer to the motel door. She doesn't seem to notice. She's not awake for it.

The knocks are gentle and spaced apart, but consistent.

That's not a rat.

I pull the covers off myself, sitting forward. From here, I can better tell where it's coming from, and it's only coming from one corner of the room. It's coming from the door itself. There's nothing on the door, I don't think. Nothing the wind could rattle in order to make that noise. No, something—or someone—is knocking in a deliberate fashion.

Even as this dawns on me I'm reluctant to climb out of bed and check. For starters, it's cold as hell. I'm wearing my oversized t-shirt and my sweat pants and *still* I can feel the cold as soon as the covers are off. I almost have half a mind to demand some kind of reimbursement for the room after sleeping in what practically feels like an icebox.

The knocking is still happening.

"What the hell," I mutter as I finally stand out of bed and tiptoe to the window. I pull the curtain back and peer out. It's too dark to see, really. Although it does appear something is out there, a dark shape on the ground I can't really make out very well. I let go of the curtain and continue to the door itself. I throw one last glance toward my grandma, sleeping none the wiser.

I open the door.

With a cold gust of wind, a dead man's hand flops across the door's threshold at my feet and I scream at the sight of him.

"Oh my God!"

I step away as if it *was* a rat lunging at my feet. In an instant there's light. My grandma, alerted by my outburst, has already turned on her bedside lamp. It's not a rat at my feet, but Jason.

"Oh my God," I repeat, this time in a tone of concern. I step into the doorway and peer out into the parking lot, scouring the dark winter storm for anyone else who might be lurking about. I don't see anything. I crouch beside Jason, collapsed and unmoving.

"J-Jason?" I stammer.

"What is it?" my grandma asks, leaning out of bed. "What's happened, Lana?"

"It's Jason. One of the men we picked up."

"What's the matter with him?"

"I… I don't know."

I glance outside once more, where my car is parked just in front of our room's door, to the surrounding lot, as deserted as ever.

"I'm gonna get him inside…"

I grab hold of Jason's arms and pull him through the doorway. A moan escapes him as I do, which tells me he's conscious, at least. I drag him to the floor at the foot of my bed. I shut the door after us, re-locking it just in case. My grandma climbs out of bed and comes to see Jason for herself in her pajamas. She puts a hand to her mouth in shock.

"Oh my. Is he… is he dead?"

"No. I don't think so."

I crouch beside him again, where his face is turned against the carpet. His mouth hangs open, his lips cracked and dry from the cold. He's got so much snow melting in his hair, his eyebrows, it gives him the appearance of an old, graying man. I draw my gaze along the rest of him, down the back of his jacket, and gasp at what I see.

"Jesus. I think he's been stabbed."

"Stabbed?"

It's quite apparent judging by the bloody wound—a wide slit through the jacket's fabric, its edges soaked with his blood.

Jason makes a noise. An unintelligible mutter. I lean closer.

"What happened to you?" I say. "Who did this?"

He blinks his eyes, which are barely opened in the first place. His gaze is distant. Foggy. I think he's hanging on by a thread.

"Shit."

I jump to my feet. I grab my phone off my nightstand and check its signal. Unsurprisingly I'm still not getting any service out here. I cross the room to the wired telephone on the long dresser. I pick up the receiver and put it to my ear. There's no dial tone. I push a few of the buttons and listen. Still nothing.

"Are you fucking kidding me?"

"What is it?"

I shake my head, annoyed. "The phone's not working. I'm gonna go get help. Stay here with him, okay?"

My grandma shrugs, as if to say *'what else could I possibly do?'*

I stuff my feet into my boots and lace them up as quickly as I can. Then I throw my puffy white coat on. I look like a frumpy mess in my sweat pants, but I guess now's not the time to be shallow.

"Be careful," my grandma says. "Whoever did this is probably still out there."

"It was probably his own *buddy*," I say, emphasizing Jason's own word. "I told you these guys were bad news from the moment we first picked them up."

I pull my hood over my head and step out into the cold dark. I shut the door behind me. Then I pause there on the walkway, surveying the rest of the parking lot. There's still only my car and the truck parked behind the manager's house. I gaze toward Jason's room along the other stretch of motel room doors. Is his companion in there now? Could it have been him? An ultimate betrayal? A *literal* backstab?

There's no one else out here that I can see. I hurry across the lot, kicking snow, hugging myself tightly, throwing the odd glance at Room 3's door as I go. It's freezing. The snowfall seems to have thinned, but only a little. It's still coming down. I turn the corner of the manager's house, into the eerie glow of that bright red roadside sign, and a worrisome thought occurs to me.

Has she discovered the missing money yet?

It's a little late to be worrying about that, I'm aware. But I worry all the same. Will she know it was me? Will any of that even matter once I inform her there's a dying man inside our motel room? Or that there's a possible killer on the loose?

I'm so deep in my worries that I forget it's after eleven now as I try the front door. But it doesn't matter. The door is unlocked. I push inside, dinging the overhead doorbell. Throwing all courtesy out the window, I beeline for the front desk, for the little bell there, and proceed to ding it incessantly for a good twenty seconds or so. Then I stand back, peer toward the head of the stairs, and call loudly to whomever might hear me.

JASPER

*E*verything hurts again. I think whatever painkillers she's given me have worn off, or are starting to wear off. That or the pain itself is getting worse, rising above the drug-altered baseline. My cheek stings where she slapped me.

And scratched me. She fucking scratched me.

I was so exhausted by my previous escape attempt, I could hardly fight back or defend myself from her temper tantrum. Now she's gone. She's been gone for a while. I thought I could hear her before, close by. The sounds of whimpering. Sobbing. They have since faded, however.

I lay in my growing aches and pains in complete silence.

Quentin is dead. She killed him. I'm afraid she'll kill me too before the night is through. Maybe with violence, or maybe the poison she's already fed me will finish doing its job. I don't feel so sedated anymore, at least. I no longer feel as though I'm constantly fending off sleep. But my body hurts and my muscles are so fatigued it's hard to find the willpower to move. I am sapped of strength.

And then the bell downstairs starts to ring again.

Ding, ding, ding, ding, ding.

And a voice calls out, *"Hello?"*

It's a woman's voice, but not hers. A stranger's voice. Somebody innocent, I think. Someone who might help me.

Now's my chance. I just have to move again.

I want to yell out in reply, to call for help, but it comes out hoarse and strangled in the back of my throat.

"Help," I say, my voice as flaccid as my body. "Help…"

I can't even properly shout.

I have to hold my breath to sit upright. Somehow, as my thoughts become clearer, my body becomes that much more drained. Lethargic. I repeat the same process I'd already accomplished before, swiveling my legs out of bed. Maybe this time I'll make it farther than the nightstand before fucking everything up.

I can do this.

I think I can do this.

Sitting on the edge of the bed with my feet touching the floor, I glimpse my naked torso now the scratchy wool sweater has been removed. I'm bleeding through my bandages. A lot. When did that start? Was it when she pinned me down before with her knee on my stomach? There's no way to know. But that's where I hurt the most. It almost hurts as much now as it did before in Quentin's truck, before I ever pulled into this place. Did my stitches come undone? Is something terribly wrong with me? I was already running on borrowed time before. How much time do I have left?

My wound sings as I repeat the ordeal of standing out of bed for the second time. I use the nightstand for support like before, but this time I'm much more careful about it. Even so, as I sway onto my feet I can't stop from freezing up in sheer pain. It feels like my guts are about to spill out of me, like the bandage around my stomach is the only thing holding them in. Excruciating.

I push away from the nightstand. My footing is unsteady. My legs threaten to buckle. I stumble toward the wall and catch myself there, bracing against it with my forearm.

Slowly but surely, I begin shuffling my way toward the bedroom door.

DARLENE

*L*ana's gone for help, leaving me with the dying man on our motel room floor. Jason. He's lying face down on the carpet. I want to roll him over, but judging by the wound in his back I'm not sure that's a good idea. I'd hate to hurt him any more than he's already hurting. Instead I grab my jacket and it drape it over him. Then I kneel beside him while we wait for Lana's return.

He's still alive. His eyes are barely open, barely blinking. His breath leaves his parted mouth in ragged gasps.

"Hold on, dear," I tell him. "Help is coming."

What else can I do for him? He looks as though he's ready to give up the ghost any second. I'm not sure *anything* can be done for him at this point, truth be told. And if I'm being especially truthful, I've placed my jacket over his body as much to keep him warm as I've done it so that I no longer have to see that terrible, bloody hole in his jacket. The sight of him pains me.

As we wait, he moves his lips but his voice is nonexistent. He blinks his eyes drearily.

"What is it?" I ask him. I lean closer. "What do you want to say, Jason?"

His lips continue to tremble, opening and closing without a sound. He wishes to say something, I just know it, but he lacks the vigor.

"I'm sorry?" I lean in closer. "Say it again, Jason. Tell me."

"The…" The word leaves his lips like a ghost itself. Soft, without edges.

"Go on…"

"The… woman…"

"The woman?"

"The woman…"

I'm leaning so close that I feel his final breath on my cheek, dry and tepid. Rattling. His dying breath. Then he goes still. His eyes remain partly open, but the difference is staggering—between life and death.

No longer a dying man, but a dead one.

MISSY

I've cried myself into a serene, sleepy stupor when the bell starts to ring. It startles me upright. Sitting on our bed, I peer about the dark room, confused, anxious. How could someone be ringing the bell when it's well past—

Oh.

I could slap myself for being so thick skulled. In my rage, in my wrathful return from Room 3, I've left the door unlocked. Now someone is down there, ringing away. There's only one guest it could be, I'm well aware.

The thief.

"Hello?"

Her shouting voice travels up the stairs through our bedroom doorway like an alarm. A droning, bothersome alarm I wish to smash to pieces and silence forever. But I can't do that, of course. It's only wishful thinking. A private jest. I've already collected enough bodies tonight, haven't I? I wipe what few tears have yet to dry off my cheeks and stand up in the dark. I straighten my clothes about my body. I take a deep breath.

Let this be over quickly.

I hurry to meet her. I adopt an expression of great concern as I descend the stairs, as well as an ounce of feigned confusion for her being here.

"I'm sorry," she starts to say before I interrupt her.

"I thought I locked the door."

She looks fleetingly at the door over her shoulder. "I actually tried calling before I came, but the phone wasn't working, or I couldn't get it to work, anyway…"

"Oh, I'm sorry about that. Our system can be finicky sometimes. I'll have to take a look…"

"There's been an attack," the young woman blurts out. It's only now I notice the state of her, the pallor of her skin, the wild exhaustion in her eyes.

"An attack?"

"The man I arrived here with," she says, and my stomach drops into a cold, acidic pit somewhere along my pelvic floor. "He… he showed up outside our door. I don't think he can even walk. He can barely speak. I think somebody attacked him. I… I think it might've been…"

She trails off as though she doesn't wish to say. Uncertain. Getting ahead of herself, perhaps?

"Attacked?" I ask. It's all I can manage to say myself. My own thoughts are scattered. I don't know how it's possible. I feel like I'm dreaming, like this is some kind of nightmare—one of those awfully awkward scenarios in which you embarrass yourself in some socially irredeemable way.

I've been caught.

But I haven't. He can barely speak, she said. Not to mention if she knew the truth of it all, she would hardly come to *me* to report it!

"Yes, I think he's been stabbed. We have to call the police."

It's that singular word that snaps me back to planet earth. *Police.* No way, Jose. I can't have that. I can have exactly *none* of that.

"Oh my goodness," I say. "Did he say who attacked him?"

"No. I don't think he could..." She trails off again before shaking her head. "I would have called the police myself but my phone doesn't get service out here. Maybe with the storm and everything, I don't know..."

Thank God, is all I can think. I feel as though I've been pulled away from the ledge of a fatal drop by a mere half-inch of my heel. *Thank God for storms. Thank God for unreliable cell service. Just... thank God.*

"I was thinking about going and checking on his friend, but—"

"No!" I say, my voice more forceful than I intend. "It could be dangerous. Just... go back to your room and stay with your grandmother. Please. I'll check their room... right after I call the police."

The young woman appears relieved to hear this, though there's still an obvious doubt plaguing her. For a moment she seems stuck, unsure what to do. I'm reminded of her earlier warning, about keeping an eye on Jason. *Quentin.* I wonder if she's reflecting on that now as well.

"Okay," she says at last, her gears turning all the while. "Just... be careful."

Finally she leaves. The door dings and she's gone. I have no intention of calling the police, of course. Instead I hurry to the kitchen, to the curtain drawn across the sliding glass door. I peek out and watch as she crosses through the parking lot back to her room. Quentin's in there right now. *Alive,* somehow. I pray he can't speak. I pray he can't tell them what's happened. If things get too out of hand—if that young woman and her grandmother become liabilities —they'll leave me no choice.

I've never in my life felt so entangled by loose ends. It's an incredible feat just to prioritize my next step.

How the hell is he still alive?

I can't dwell on that. I need to keep my remaining guests calm. I need a convincing story, something to buy me time, at least enough to last me until tomorrow morning when I can hopefully send them on their way.

The police are stretched thin after the storm last night, but they'll be coming later in the afternoon. You're both free to go in the meantime. They won't be needing statements from either of you. Promise.

I've still got my jacket on. And my boots. I wonder what that young woman must have thought, watching me come downstairs all sleepy-eyed but still dressed for the outdoors. Hopefully she was too distracted to notice. She seemed plenty preoccupied.

I start for the front door, but as I reach the lobby I'm stopped by a noise upstairs. A singular creak. I crane my neck and listen. A gust of wind hits the house and sends the whole place groaning. Perhaps that's all I'd heard. The wind.

I step outside and hastily head toward Room 3, pulling

my chunky ring of keys from my pocket along the way. My jacket pocket still jostles with the weight of Quentin's handgun. I glance discreetly in the direction of the others' room, Room 16. Their window is alight, but I don't see anyone peering out. I imagine they're busy with him at the moment.

God help them if he talks.

I move to unlock the door to Room 3 and realize I never locked it after my previous visit. Again, I could slap myself. How could I be so careless?

Fortunately the man called Allen is still quite dead. He lies exactly where I left him. The blood is even grislier than I remember it. A true horror. The sight of his opened throat makes me tense, makes me *hurt.* I did that to him. It's hard to believe—as though that'd been someone else's dirty work, someone else's eyes I'd only peered through for a time.

It's amazing, really, discovering what we're capable of…

Now it's time for me to come up with my story.

JASPER

I hear another bell ring just as I reach the bedroom door. Just one little jingle. I think it must have been the bell over the door downstairs.

Right now all I can worry about is the door in front of me. It's a challenge to keep standing as I open it. I need to brace myself against the wall to stay upright, while also needing the strength to step into the doorway as I push it open. Each step I take is a dangerous one, my legs and ankles quivering as I settle my weight from one foot onto the next. I finally emerge into the hallway. The house is quiet. No more voices. No more dinging bell. It seems the woman I heard before is gone.

I stagger ahead on brave feet. I keep a single hand to the wall for guidance, for balance. I pause, taking a deep but quiet breath, mustering what little endurance I have left. I pass an open door on my right. It's dark. I only glance in as I stumble from one side of the door frame to the other. It's another bedroom. The master bedroom. *Her* bedroom. I continue along the hall, shuffling, shaking, until I reach the head of the stairs, which opens into the high-ceilinged lobby before me.

I glimpse her as she's making her way to the front door. I duck aside, out of sight. The floor creaks under my foot as I do.

Shit.

Her footsteps pause down below. I hold my breath. Did she hear that?

An enormous gust of wind sweeps about the house, creaking and groaning. The bell over the door dings once again as she departs. Then the house is entirely still. Entirely empty. Except for me. I let out the breath I was holding and shudder with it.

I square myself up to the head of the stairs. The descent is daunting, but I have no choice. I grab hold of the wooden stair railing and take my first wobbly step down. It feels as though I'm shaking less than when I first stood out of bed, like my muscles are catching up, my blood pumping. Even still, I take the stairs slowly. I can't mess up now. Help is close. Too close to fall short.

At the bottom stair, a cramp in my gut doubles me over. I hold onto the railing, fighting back the urge to scream, the pain is so intense. The blood that's soaked through my bandages has since started dribbling down the rest of my abdomen, absorbing into the waistband of my boxer shorts.

They're not my boxer shorts, I remind myself, as petty a distinction as it may be.

The pain subsides. Or lessens. I stand mostly straight again. Standing *too* straight sends another ripping twinge through me, like my body is pulling apart at the seams. I move past the foot of the stairs to the front desk, where I first signed in upon my arrival. There's a corded phone on the wall. I scurry there as quickly as my gelatin feet will carry me. I unhook the phone from its cradle and put it to my ear, but there's no sound. No dial tone. Has she disconnected the lines? I hang the phone back up and keep moving. I have to keep moving. I perform a quick search of the desk, lined with so many empty cubbies. I'm hoping to find the keys to Quentin's truck, but there's not a lot to see here. Where would she have hidden them?

There's a light on down the hall. I move around the desk, into the hallway where I see the kitchen at the other end. Keeping to the wall, I slide my way there. Each step jiggles my insides. Tiny, needling spasms. The first thing my eyes happen upon is the duffel bag on the kitchen table. The money. *My* money.

That's the last thing you should be worrying about.

I know this. I might not be the brightest bulb, but I'm not an idiot. I ignore the money and scour the kitchen for keys. Instead, what I notice next is the cutlery block on the kitchen counter with a knife already missing. I'd wager that's the knife in Quentin's back. I grab the knife from the next slot. Smaller, but still dangerous. Good to have, just in case.

Failing to find the truck keys, the only other place I can think to look would be in the woman's bedroom. I've heard her go in there several times over the course of the night, after all.

I return to the lobby, to the foot of the stairs, and realize how much more daunting the climb is than the descent. My poor legs turn watery at just the thought.

I suppose I could simply flee the house and start yelling,

run into the parking lot and make a commotion and hope the other guests hear me. Is that an option? And what if I run into *her* the moment I set foot outside? She'll pounce on me before I can even find my voice.

I'm running out of time.

I begin climbing the stairs. My footing is clumsy, but I manage them well enough, fast enough, using the handrail to pull myself up step by step. By the time I reach the top, my stomach is on fire. Pulsing. I'm out of breath. I could really use a glass of water. I hobble into her dark bedroom. I avoid the overhead light, not wanting to draw any attention if she happens to see it from outside. I cross immediately to the bed, then to the nightstand beside it. I flip on the lamp. It's probably not any safer than turning on the bright ceiling light, but oh well.

There's a long dresser along the wall. I pull open its drawers one after the other, revealing socks and underwear and folded up pants, as well as an odd drawer full of baseball caps. No keys. Nothing. I turn in place. My eyes return to the nightstand with the lamp. I stumble there again. I slide the top drawer open and find a pair of eyeglasses, a bottle of vitamins, an orange prescription bottle of something else. My eyes linger upon that orange bottle. I know whatever's inside is probably what's responsible for my current state. Possibly. It doesn't matter at this point, I suppose.

I shut the drawer, open the one underneath… and gasp at what I find.

LANA

My grandma looks up to see me as I enter our motel room and her eyes are brimming with tears. The man on the floor—Jason—is covered by her jacket. And dead. I can tell at just a glance. His eyes are partly open. But he's dead.

"He died just after you left," my grandma says. "Did you call for help?"

"The manager is calling the police right now."

"What about Carl? Someone should check on him."

"She's gonna check their room right after she calls the police, but…" I hesitate. "…for all we know, Grandma, he's the one who did this."

My grandma cocks her head in confusion.

"Carl?" she says, as if she's known the guy her whole life. "No, this wasn't him."

"You sat in a car together for a couple hours tops. You don't know the first thing about these people."

"He didn't strike me as the type who would do something like this."

"Who else do you think might have done it, then? This motel isn't exactly bustling, is it? There are two cars in the parking lot and one of them's ours."

"I don't know," my grandma says. "It just doesn't feel right." She takes a deep breath, a thought visibly forming behind her gaze."He said something to me just before he died. He said... *the woman.* That's it. *'The woman.'* I know that could mean a lot of things, but..."

"But what?"

My grandma's attention rests on Jason's body, on his back in particular where she's so graciously draped her jacket.

"Didn't you say the manager's a woman?" my grandma says.

I already know what she's asking. What she's *really* asking.

"He wasn't referring to her."

"Is there anyone else he might've been referring to?"

"I don't know, *me?* I'd just left the room, after all. Besides, he was on the brink of death. He was probably confused. Like you said, he could have meant anything by that."

My grandma shakes her head doubtfully.

"He was stabbed in the back," I go on. "Whoever did this had to get the jump on him, right? And who else could've done that besides his own buddy Carl?"

"His brother, you mean."

"No, that was just part of Jason's made-up story when you asked them where they were headed."

My grandma looks at me like I'm crazy. "You've watched far too many of those murder movies..."

"They're called documentaries. They're real. And so is what I'm telling you. Check this out…"

I grab my grandma's jacket and toss it onto the bed. Then I grab Jason by the shoulder and, before I *truly* understand that I'm handling a corpse, I flip him over onto his back. My grandma gasps.

"Lana!"

I unzip Jason's jacket and throw it open, revealing the gun holster still attached to his side. Except now the holster is empty.

"What on earth are you doing?" my grandma laments. "This is a dead body. You can't just… This is *evidence…*"

"He had a gun before. See that? It's a holster."

"And what's that got to do with anything?"

"Jason and Carl are thugs, Grandma. You didn't pick up on that? At all? I guess you wouldn't…"

"You're being ridiculous. Now put him back the way he was. Hurry."

I roll my eyes, but do as she says. I zip up his jacket, tracing my hand with my gaze until I'm looking him in the face. His cold, dead-eyed face. I flip him back over where he was before. My grandma can't help gasping again, appalled.

"I can't believe you…"

"Relax, Grandma. He's dead."

"And you should *respect* the dead. Don't you know that's what this whole trip is about?"

I let out a great big sigh. It's all I can do. If I say anything else, I'll only get myself into more trouble, I'm sure.

"I'm sorry," I say. And I mean it. My grandma looks

hurt, and I'm well aware it hardly has anything to do with Jason. I stand up, unsure what else to say. I'm itching to get out of here, to escape this conversation and the dead man on our motel room floor. "I could use another smoke…"

"Oh, I wish you wouldn't. You know that's why your grandpa had such a hard time with his…"

She's interrupted by a knock on our door. We both exchange glances with one another. After a brief hesitation, I answer it. The motel manager stands just outside, her arms wrapped tightly around herself in the blowing cold. I stand aside to let her in.

"Oh, God," she says as she sees the body on the floor. "Is he…"

"He's dead," my grandma answers. "He passed just a few moments ago."

"You called the police, then?" I ask.

The manager doesn't answer right away, her attention fixated on the corpse.

"I did, but…" She appears to have to *tear* her gaze away in order to focus on me instead. "With the weather like it is, it might be a while before anyone shows up. I guess there's a surge of accidents, so they're stretched thin."

"But this is a *murder*," my grandma says. "You'd think that'd take priority…"

The manager only shrugs, as her eyes are drawn back to the dead body, unable to leave it.

"What about the other guy?" I say. "Did you check?"

"I did. He wasn't in their room."

"Wasn't in their room?" my grandma echoes. "Where else could he be?"

"Well, that's just it," the manager goes on. "Their room

was entirely empty. But I *did* find blood on the carpet, as well as recent footprints outside their door, leading toward the road."

"Toward the road?"

"Yes. I can't say for certain, but it would seem his partner may have been responsible."

I can't help feeling a little vindicated by the manager's suspicions. My grandma looks skeptical as ever.

Then something else occurs to me. I nod toward the body on the floor.

"I saw him heading toward your place earlier tonight. Did you talk to him?"

The manager tilts her head curiously, eyes narrowing, before ultimately shaking her head *no*.

"I haven't spoken to him since he checked in," she says. "Was this before or after you came for your blankets?"

"After."

The manager thinks on that a bit, then nods with under-standing.

"That would make sense, actually…"

She looks me dead in the eyes now, and though I can't expressly say *why*, her expression is different than it was, charged with something I can't immediately place.

"Earlier tonight, I noticed it looked as though someone had been in my house, like someone had gone through some of my things downstairs. Perhaps that had been him."

She says all of this without breaking eye contact with me, and it's all I can do to resist squirming under her gaze. Is she referring to the money? Does she know it was me? Surely she can't, she *can't*, but the suspicion is undoubtedly there. I furrow my brow in what I hope looks like genuine confusion.

"Maybe," I say.

"Who else is here?" my grandma interjects. "Any other guests spending the night?"

"I have one other guest in Room 19. But he arrived much earlier and hasn't left his room, as far as I know."

My grandma frowns, looking doubtful as she rests her sorry eyes on Jason's body.

The manager produces a formidable ring of keys from her pocket, and begins sorting through them one by one.

"I'm so terribly sorry about all of this, but I'd like to leave him exactly as he is, for the police. Could I offer you two another room in the meantime?"

"Of course we'll take another room," I answer.

What else are we going to do, I wonder? Sleep in here with a corpse?

"If you'd gather your things and follow me," she says, finally settling on one of the keys she's been searching through. "I'll take you over to Room 7. It's got two beds the same as this one."

"That's wonderful," my grandma says. "Thank you."

"Do you need help carrying anything?"

"We've got it," I say. "We'll meet you over there."

I give the manager a weak smile, urging her to go on ahead of us. After a short-lived staring contest, she gets the idea and leaves us to it. I turn around and my grandma is already packing up her bathroom supplies and whatever else, stuffing her things haphazardly back into her bag. It's strange, watching her go through the motions of something so *ordinary* with something so terribly *extraordinary* still lying on the floor between us.

"So… Carl's gone missing."

"Oh, hush." my grandma avoids looking at me altogether. "I still don't think it sounds right. Not one bit of it…"

I chew my lip, thinking it over myself rather than gathering my things like I should be doing. I watch as my grandma packs up my grandpa's urn, making a kind of nest for it amongst her folded clothes.

"I have to admit, it does sound a little far-fetched," I say. "Mostly because we know Carl could hardly walk on that leg of his."

"Exactly!" my grandma says as she slams her luggage bag shut, wide-eyed and satisfied by my own suspicion. "It doesn't make any sense at all, does it? How could Carl have done… *that*, in his condition?"

She gestures to Jason's body as she says this.

"Yeah. I don't know."

I make quick work of packing up my own things. My grandma slips into her coat and boots before we head outside. I shut the door behind us, then peer toward the other half of the motel, where Room 7's door is wide open, the light on, waiting. I stick close to my grandma, afraid she'll slip on the ice. The manager is inside when we get there, stepping out of the bathroom, making sure everything's ready for us.

"I hope this is all right," she says, as we each dump our bags at the ends of the beds. "I'll go fetch the guest key while you two get settled in. I'll be right back."

The manager hurries outside and shuts us into the

silence of our new-but-identical room. I can't help thinking how strange this all feels. I can't explain it. Someone was just *murdered,* and yet there's a distinct lack of urgency to the situation.

"Surreal," I say, trying the word out for myself as it occurs to me.

"You say something?" my grandma says behind me, overhearing.

"Nothing."

I turn and watch as she begins unmaking her new bed. Then she pauses, remembering something. I remember in the same instant.

"The extra blankets," I say, beating her to the punch. "I'll go get 'em."

I return outside, moving swiftly along the length of the motel back to Room 16. Doing my best to ignore the corpse still lying on the floor, I quickly pull the extra blankets off from each of the beds, gathering them into a huge bundle in my arms. I glance at Jason only once on my way out. His eyes are still open in that inexplicably disturbing way. I've seen that look before. The look of the dead. I have to resist the resulting shiver that travels up my spine.

Closing the door behind me, I stop for a moment and regard the snowy ground at my feet, where Jason had been lying when I discovered him knocking outside our door. I can still see the trail his body made in the snow when he crawled here—and it isn't coming from Room 3. It leads in the opposite direction, into the empty fields beyond the property. How does that make any sense?

"What the hell…"

I stare in that direction, unsure what to make of it. Then

finally I return to my grandma with the blankets. I set the whole pile on the end of her bed and simply stand there for a time, consumed in thought.

"What is it?" she asks, noticing my vacant expression.

"I don't know. Something just doesn't..."

I startle as there comes a knock on our door. That would be her again. I try and steel my nerves as I answer the door and find the manager already extending the new room key in her hand to me.

"Here's this," she says. It's just like the first key, except this one's little wooden fob says 7. "Again, I'm so sorry about all of this. I... I've never had to deal with anything like this before."

"Yeah, no, for sure." I struggle to sound authentic as I say it. I take the key from her... and as I do, I finally realize why all of this feels so *off*.

It's her. *She's* off. There's been a murder on her property and she's...

Too calm? Too collected? Too hospitable?

I suppose maybe she's just very good at her job. She might be panicking on the inside while she maintains a sturdy exterior for our sake. Yeah, I guess that's possible, too. But even still, it feels strange to be apologized to in this way, as if we've been moved to a new room due to some technical malfunction rather than a cold-blooded murder.

"I'm going to try and get the phones working again," she adds. "But in the meantime, I would really appreciate it if you could both try to remain in your room the rest of the night. There's no telling for certain where that man's attacker disappeared to..."

"Killer," I say, correcting her. I don't know why I do it,

really, but I do. It feels wrong to call it something else. Maybe that's my grandma's righteousness seeping into me. "His killer."

"Right…" The manager avoids looking me in the eye again. Instead she steps back, clears her throat, and says, "I'll let you know if anything major comes up."

I stand in the doorway and watch her go. She looks over her shoulder once as she reaches her home, as if she feels me watching. Then she disappears around the corner.

"Close the door," my grandma says. "You're letting the cold in."

"I'm gonna smoke one last time before bed. I need it."

I step outside and shut the door before my grandma has a chance to argue with me about it. I take out my lighter and another smoke. I watch the surrounding shadows closely, as difficult as it is with the snow still flurrying down. I don't think it's going to stop tonight.

I peer toward my car, still parked in front of Room 16. I can see the snow creeping up the tires, five or six inches deep by now. I don't remember how deep it was when we first got here…

I take my first drag and it's nicotine heaven. I hold it a few seconds, blow it out. My shoulders ease down from around my neck. I take another drag. I need it even more than the first. As I breathe it in deep, I peer in the other direction, along this length of the motel. Toward Room 3.

Blowing out another cloud of chemicals, I let my curiosity get the better of me.

I walk the distance between Room 7 and Room 3, watching the house the whole way, the *Main Office*, my mind spinning yarns faster than my own grandma could crochet them. There's a niggling doubt in the back of my mind I can't shake. I think my grandma put it there.

The woman...

Jason's apparent last words toll around the bell of my skull.

I arrive outside Room 3's door, where I can still make out a clutter of footprints coming and going. Jason's and the manager's most recently, I assume. The larger footprints, Jason's earlier footprints, are still visible even if they've already filled with new snow.

As far as I can tell, every recent set of footprints either links between here and the Main Office, or between here and Room 16 across the parking lot. The latter would be the manager's, coming to see us after checking on Room 3, like she said she did.

My heart has since started pounding. I take yet another drag on my cigarette, but it doesn't help.

Contrary to the manager's story, there's not a single footprint leading toward the road that I can see.

JASPER

*W*hat I find in the bottom drawer of the nightstand petrifies me.

Wallets. So many wallets. The drawer is literally full of them. A couple dozen, *at least.* I spot mine immediately, as well as my phone and the keys to Quentin's truck. I take them out, set them on top of the nightstand to separate them from the rest. I set the kitchen knife on the nightstand as well and, out of pure morbid curiosity, I grab another wallet. This one belongs to Quentin. I grab another. It belongs to a man by the name of *Nathan Greenfield.* I grab another. *Corbin Schultz.* Another. *Terry Hoffman.*

Who are all these men and why are their wallets all stashed in the motel manager's nightstand drawer? Why am I asking myself questions I already know the answers to?

I'm next.

I grab my phone off the nightstand. I wake it up, unlock it with my thumbprint. Miraculously I have cell service—a single sliver. My heart is fucking *pounding* against my ribcage, reverberating through me, my guts throbbing hot and sour with each beat.

I begin dialing when the bell over the door dings downstairs. My racing heart strikes the back of my throat. She's returned. I freeze. Listen. Within seconds, the bell dings once again and everything is silent. I think she's left again. I let out a tremored breath and dial for help.

9-1-1.

I'm a criminal, I know that, but suddenly being arrested doesn't seem so bad. Preferable to this hell. Being arrested is better than dying, right?

"Nine-one-one, what's your…"

The dispatcher—a woman's voice—cuts off and I never hear the end of her greeting. I take my phone away from my ear and discover the call's ended. My sliver of service is gone.

"Fuck you." I dial the number again. I put the phone to my ear. A lovely, robotic voice informs me that I'm unable to connect my call. *"Fuck you!"*

I grab my wallet and keys and the kitchen knife from the nightstand and stand up once again, maybe a little too abruptly as my stomach protests with a slicing pain from front to back. I clench my teeth, turn for the bedroom door. I return to the stairs. Even in just the last couple minutes, my faculties seem to have recovered substantially. My muscles still ache and I can't help moving like a slug, but it's more to do with the pain now than an inability to control myself. I descend the stairs, wincing every step. I move to the front door and stop myself. If I go through the front, I'll have to circle the whole house. I'm more likely to be caught that way, I think. Whereas I'm parked out back near the sliding door. Hopefully she hasn't moved the truck already. This would all be hopeless if she has.

I make my way back into the kitchen. Since I'm already here, I open the duffel bag on the table and toss my wallet and phone inside. I sling the bag's strap over my shoulder, much to the suffering of my various gunshot wounds.

The bell over the front door jingles yet again. I freeze by the kitchen table, out of sight from anyone peering down the hallway. I listen intently until I hear her stomping her way upstairs. I don't have much time. I hurry to the back door. I pull the curtain aside, flip the latch on the sliding door's handle.

"Jasper?" her voice echoes from above.

She's just discovered my empty bed. I have seconds now. I yank on the sliding door.

"What the…"

The door slides a half inch before jamming up on something. I pull the curtain further aside and discover the wooden rod blocking the track. Of course.

"Jasper!"

Her footsteps return to the stairs, stomping down.

I bend over and nearly cry out from the pain. I grab the wooden rod, pull it loose, toss it to the floor. I stand again, my wound *ripping* under my bandages. That's what it feels like, anyway. Ripping. I grab the door handle and yank it wide open, the harsh breath of winter pressing against my half-naked body, covering me in goosebumps.

"Jasper, wait!" she screams from the end of the hallway, hurrying after me.

In nothing but boxer shorts, with the truck keys in one hand, a knife in the other, and my bag slung over my shoulder, I step outside into the freezing cold.

MISSY

I've successfully moved the women into another room with minimal complaints and given them good reason to stay there without asking too many questions. I do think they might be wary of my story, however. There are holes, I'm aware. But there's insufficient reason to disbelieve it altogether. I think I'm finally getting a handle on things.

That is, until I discover the guest bedroom door wide open.

I'm hollowed out in an instant. I glide into the doorway, walking on nightmarish clouds as all sensation leaves my body, the last of my nerves fraying like rope. I already know what I'm about to find.

Jasper's bed is empty.

"Jasper?" I call, spinning on my heel.

I return down the hall, pausing in my bedroom doorway. I peer inside and my eyes latch onto my nightstand, the lamp turned on, the bottom drawer still open. He's gone through my things. He's found *his* things. He's getting away.

"Jasper!"

I spin on my heel once more, dashing for the stairs, down the stairs, my boots clomping. He couldn't have gotten far. I haven't been gone long at all, and I've been coming in and out all the while. He would have had to time his exit perfectly, and that's not to mention his faculties, or lack thereof. I would have seen him at some point.

He couldn't have gotten far.

I hurry into the hallway, heading for the kitchen, and see him. My heart soars. Nauseating. The sliding door is open and he's stepping outside. He's getting away.

Getting away, getting away…

"Jasper, wait!"

I run. I chase. I reach the sliding door just as he's reached the truck parked there, stuffing the key into the door, trying to unlock it, to twist it. I advance without thinking, without considering. I reach for him, moving through the cold dark, the kitchen's light at my back throwing my shadow across the parking lot.

"Jasper, stop. Please. What are you—"

I grab him by the arm and suddenly he turns, *lashes,* and something stings me.

"Get away from me!" he screeches.

I recoil from him, two steps, boots sliding through the snow and ice. I bring my left hand in, cradled in the other, and observe the fresh blood filling up my palm where he's sliced me. He leans against the truck door, his whole body trembling, his hand trembling most of all as he extends the kitchen knife in my direction. A threat. A warning.

"Stay away," he says. His voice quivers as much as he

does. "I'm leaving. Do you hear me? I'm leaving. Let me go. Just… just let me go."

"Geoffrey…" I start to say, and recognize the mistake as soon as I speak it.

"My name isn't *fucking* Geoffrey," he spits.

"Jasper, please. You're not…"

"I know what you are!" he screams, and his voice is punchier than I'd like. Loud. Strong. It's as if the drugs haven't had half the effect on him as they should. "I know what you are. You're… you're crazy… you're…"

I look beyond him, scanning the rear stretch of the motel, my eyes lingering on Room 16 before I remember they're not there anymore, they're in Room 7, whose door I can't see from here with the truck parked between it and myself. I fear they'll hear his screams, that they'll come outside to investigate. I have to stop him. Somehow. I can still feel the weight of the gun in my jacket pocket. It's the only defense I have at this point in time. I've also still got Allen's wallet in my pocket. I never got around to putting it with the others…

"You'll never hear from me again," Jasper says, still pointing the knife my way. "Okay? Just let me go. I won't… I won't go to the police, just… let me go."

I know he's lying. He's desperate. He'll say anything to convince me. There's absolutely no chance I'm letting him climb inside that truck. He has to know that. He has to know *I* know that.

"The roads are too dangerous," I say. I suppose I'm pretty desperate as well, pretending we can both just ignore the evidence he found in my nightstand drawer and all the rest, that we can pretend everything is fine between us. "Your injuries are still too fresh. Look, you're bleeding through your bandages. You should let me take a look at your stitches before—"

"You're not coming near me!"

I wince at the volume. It's more than I can stand. I can't let him take this any further.

I reach inside my jacket pocket.

"What's going on?"

Jasper and I both flinch at the sound of another voice. I turn and see her—the slimy thief from Room 16. Room 7. Whichever. She stands just beyond the other side of the truck's hood. Why is she there? Why is she *here* at all? I notice the fresh boot prints in the snow behind her, highlighted under the functioning lamppost. She's walked here from Room 3, it appears. Conducting a little investigation of her own? After I told her to stay inside?

Nosy little—

"Please!" Jasper looks to the woman like she's going to save him somehow, as if she's the one with a gun in her pocket. "You've gotta help me…"

"What's going on?" the young woman repeats. She moves closer, her eyes darting between Jasper and me, lingering on him as she absorbs his pathetic, half-naked condition.

Jasper starts to speak again but I make sure to interrupt him this time.

"This man," I say, speaking as forcefully as I can to drown out Jasper's words, "showed up at my motel tonight on death's doorstep. He'd been shot, and—"

"This woman is keeping me here!" Jasper shouts, interrupting me just the same. "She won't let me leave! She's—"

"This man is a criminal on the run!" I shout right back, louder and louder and louder, as loud as I have to be in order to be heard. "I've revived him from near-fatal injuries. I patched him up as best I could after he—"

"*She's a murderer!*" Jasper's words ring out deafeningly, muting everything in their wake—me, her, the very storm that continues to howl around us. "She's killed I don't even know how many—"

"He's out of his *mind*," I try to reiterate. "He's under the influence of heavy painkillers. He's not thinking clearly. He's…"

The woman looks back and forth between us with each interruption, and to my dismay she seems to be following along a little too well for her own good. She doesn't appear convinced by my words. I imagine she was snooping around Room 3 because she'd already had her own suspicions. I don't know *how,* but she sees through me. I see it in her eyes as she levels them on mine.

"Was it you, then?" she asks. "Who stabbed Jason?"

I've lost all control of the situation. Is it even possible to get it back, I wonder? My hand still rests in my jacket pocket, my fingertips playing on the grip of the gun.

"His real name was Quentin," I answer, opting for the truth for once. A little truth never hurts when you're trying to sell a lie, after all. I look between the young woman and Jasper, who at the moment appears exhausted from all his shouting. I believe he thinks he's won, that he's turned the tide, but he's wrong. "And yes. I was forced to defend myself, and Jasper here. Those men you picked up were responsible for Jasper's injuries. They were actively hunting him. It was only a coincidence that you happened to stop here and they recognized the truck Jasper *stole* from them. I did the only thing I could to stop Quentin. *I saved Jasper's life.* And then..." Here's where things get tricky, where my actions become difficult to explain. "I... I got scared. I tried to hide Quentin's body out in the fields. It was stupid, I know. I didn't realize he wasn't actually dead. That's how much of a so-called *murderer* I am..."

"So everything you told us before was a lie?" the young woman says. I'm flabbergasted that after everything I've just said, she's apparently more concerned with personal insult. "You told us you hadn't seen the guest in Room 19 since he checked in, but this is him, isn't it? And you acted surprised when I came to you about Jason... or Quentin... but you knew."

Okay, so I'm *not* gaining back control of the situation. I can see the reins slipping farther away, out of reach.

"I lied to you because I was afraid things would spiral out of control if you knew the truth. Because I was worried... I was..."

"Quentin's not the first person she's killed!" Jasper says. "She's... she's got..."

"He doesn't know what he's saying. He can barely stand, for Christ's sake. He's lost so much blood, and the painkillers in his system..."

"She's got a drawer full of men's wallets!" Jasper exclaims next.

Even I'm beginning to grow tired. Exhausted. I can hardly keep up with this unraveling narrative of mine. For a moment all I can do is shake my head.

"I don't know what he thinks he saw," I say. "You see, I'm a widow. My husband... well, I've kept many of his things upstairs in our bedroom. That's all. This man is confused, like I said. I'd planned to care for him until tomorrow morning, when I was going to take him to the hospital myself."

"You also told us you found footprints leading to the road from Room 3," the woman says, ignoring everything I've just explained to her. "But I just checked, and there aren't any. So that was a lie, too. What really happened to Quentin's partner?"

I can't think of any more lies. Not on the spot like this.

"I don't know where his partner went. I never even got to see him for myself."

The woman nods like she's listening, but I can see her mind grappling with other thoughts entirely.

"Did you know he had a leg injury?" she says. "He could barely stand, let alone walk. There's no way he took off on foot. But you said you checked their room and he was gone."

"I... I don't know what to say. I don't know what to tell you..."

"You didn't really call the police, either, did you?"

The reins aren't just out of reach, they've been set aflame. Up in smoke. I'm cornered. There's no cleaning up this mess with words anymore. No lie can save me.

"Listen to me," Jasper continues. I no longer possess the willpower to interrupt him, to argue any further. "This wasn't one man's things in a drawer. She had both mine and Quentin's wallets and countless others. *Countless others.* She's not just a murderer..."

I grasp the gun in my pocket, slipping my finger across the curved trigger. The safety is still on. Am I quick enough to toggle it off and use it, however? With Jasper's final statement, I know I'll soon have to find out.

"She's a goddamn serial killer."

LANA

I'm still looking for footprints when I hear their voices. Shouting. It sounds serious. An altercation. *Drama.* I look in their direction and vaguely see her through the powdery white—the motel manager standing near the truck parked behind her home. She's holding herself like she's just touched something hot and been burned.

I wander toward them. Curious, cautious. I can't altogether make out what they're saying. Not until someone shouts again, and I realize it's a man's voice I'm hearing.

"I know what you are!"

I'm halfway across the parking lot when I finally see him—the partial shape of him, anyway—standing on the other side of the truck. He's pointing at the manager, his finger long and accusing and—

"Oh, shit," I mumble.

It's not his finger he's pointing. He's holding a knife.

I quicken my pace until I arrive near them, keeping to this side of the truck as I stand on the walkway that separates her home from the parking lot. The man is naked. Or I think he's naked. His upper body's naked, anyway. He looks terrible—dehydrated, judging by his sinewy appearance, his skin pulled taut around his lean muscles, his cheeks hollowed. He's shivering. A bag hangs off his shoulder, and it's not just any bag, either. I recognize it as the one from the manager's kitchen table. I also notice what appears to be thick white gauze wrapped around his middle, as pale as his bloodless flesh so that I almost don't notice it at first.

"You're not coming near me!" he screams.

"What's going on?" I ask.

They both seem to jump out of their skin at the sound of my voice. The man turns to see me and his pitiable expression melts into desperation. He pleads for me to help him, and the look in his eyes sends shivers all up and down my body.

This man believes he's in mortal danger.

Trying to understand what I've just walked in on, I look to the motel manager and I see a similar but quite different expression upon her brow. Fearful, desperate, but there's something else behind her gaze. It's an emotion I recognize quite well, one I've become plenty familiar with over the years.

It's the look of someone who's been caught red-handed.

I ask once more what's going on. What follows is almost incomprehensible. They take turns shouting at me, each of them trying to scream the other down. I do my best to keep up, to hear both their sides even as they're jumbled and crazed and bursting with so much panic. I'd be lying if I said my previous suspicions didn't inform whose story I find more believable, but it also doesn't help that the manager is unable to convincingly answer my questions. She lied to us before, and I can tell she's still lying now.

If the only thing she's guilty of is self-defense, why try to hide the body in the first place?

"You didn't really call the police, either, did you?" I say.

There's blood leaking down her wrist from her clenched fist. Her other hand is jammed into her jacket pocket.

"This wasn't one man's things in a drawer," the half-naked man says. "She had both mine and Quentin's wallets and countless others. *Countless others.* She's not just a murderer… *she's a goddamn serial killer."*

My pulse thumps between my ears. The woman appears detached from this debate entirely, staring at the ground at her feet, her thoughts swimming elsewhere, circling dangerous waters.

What's she got in her jacket pocket?

She starts pulling it out when the man charges her. The bag of money falls from his shoulder, hits the snow with nary a sound. Whatever's in the woman's pocket, she struggles to pull it free, like it's caught inside, too unshapely to fit. With a glimmer of sharp metal cutting through the bitter air, the man called Jasper collides against her. They crumple into the snow. I dash around the front of the truck and find them in a squirming pile. Panting. Growling. With a well-placed boot between them, the woman kicks Jasper off herself. He sprawls onto his back. He cries out, holding himself across his bandaged stomach. The woman scrambles to her feet. Springing upright, she cries out likewise as she discovers the knife's handle protruding from her shoulder.

Holy shit, is the first thought that comes to mind.

She stands motionless, a moment of shock. Meanwhile Jasper lies shivering in the snow. I hurry to him. I offer him my hand and he takes it, squeezes me so hard a few of my knuckles crack. I put my other arm around his shoulders and help get him standing. He groans with the effort, then staggers against me, on his feet.

The woman pulls the knife from her body with an animal squeal. She holds it, admiring her own blood on its blade.

"You… you stabbed me," she says, her voice subdued, caught in a momentary stupor. "You actually…"

She blinks away her disbelief, drops the knife to the ground, and stuffs her hand back into her jacket pocket.

In my ear, Jasper states plainly, "She's got a gun."

DARLENE

*I*t's not enough that there's a murderer on the loose. Lana has to risk her health with bad habits, too, apparently. I worry so much about her, I'm certain she'll be the death of me by worry alone.

I can't go to bed until she returns.

I'm sitting upright against the headboard when I hear screams outside, and the first thought that enters my mind is: *That girl's gone and done it now.*

I don't know how many years it's been since I last moved so quickly. I bolt out of bed. My bare feet sweep the flattened carpet on my way to the door. I hear more screams. They're her screams, Lana's screams. She's calling for *me.*

"Grandma, open the door!"

I do exactly that, at precisely the right moment as I'm immediately greeted by Lana on the other side, arriving in a storm of powdery snow and huffing breaths, with a handsome, half-naked man I've never seen before clinging to her.

"Oh my goodness…"

I briskly stand aside as they push in, Lana helping the strange man into our room. I peer out into the night, into the ongoing storm as Lana urges me to close the door. That's when I see her out there—the motel manager. She's moving toward us, her dark shape obscured through the snow, against the flickering light of the lamppost behind her.

"Close the door!" Lana screams a second time.

Something goes *pop.* I see it flash in the woman's hands. A gun. I flinch later than I should—these old reflexes of mine aren't what they used to be. I slam the door shut, turn the lock, and latch the chain. Meanwhile Lana dumps the half-naked man onto the end of her bed, sitting heavily with his arm clasped across his stomach where I see there are bandages wrapped around him.

"Oh my goodness, Lana…"

"Hold that thought." She moves to the long dresser and begins dragging it away from the wall toward the front door, heaving it little by little across the carpet.

"Lana, what are you—"

"She's got her own set of keys!" Lana shouts, and I understand in an instant.

I consider helping her drag the dresser, but I know for a fact I'll only injure my brittle self. She drags it before the door, then hurries to its opposite end just as the doorknob clicks, turns, and the door opens inward. It catches on its chain. Lana shoves the end of the dresser, slides it abruptly against the door, slamming it shut once again on the woman on the other side. Lana braces herself there for a moment, hands upon the dresser's surface, shoulders heaving tiredly.

"What is going on?" I look between Lana and the wounded man sitting at the foot of the bed. "Who is he?"

Before Lana can answer, there comes a series of loud, pounding knocks on the door, followed by the manager's screaming voice on the other side.

"Open the door!" When none of us say a word, or move an inch, she adds, *"This is all a huge misunderstanding! Please!"*

"She just shot a gun at us!" I exclaim.

It's only then I wonder if I've been shot. I was standing plainly in the doorway, after all. I look down at myself, studying my silk pajamas which appear unmarred by any bullets or blood. I look at Lana. She looks fine for the most part, aside from being out of breath. I peer over my shoulder, a fleeting, curious glance, and my eyes happen upon a singular dark spot in the wall of our motel room. I go to it, put my finger to the fresh hole in the wall, the bullet lodged inside.

"Oh my goodness…" I turn about on my heel, furious as the full reality of this situation finally finds me. "Lana?"

Lana sighs with exhaustion, still leaning against the dresser. The wounded man, whoever he is, seems unfazed by us, consumed for the moment by his own agonizing injuries.

"You were right," Lana says, looking at him but speaking to me. "It was her. She killed Jason. Or Quentin, was his real name, I guess. I think she killed Carl, too."

"Allen," the wounded man says, straining to speak over the pain. "The other one's name was Allen…"

My thoughts are positively *scattered.* I don't know what to make of any of this.

"And who are you?" I ask.

With his head hung low, the half-naked man lifts his gaze only enough to see me for a moment, before he winces and clenches his jaw.

"Jasper," he manages to say. "And I think I'm dying…"

He hunches forward more than he already is, so far forward that he starts to slide off the end of the bed before Lana catches him just in the nick of time. She props him upright, or tries to. Unable to hold himself up any longer, Jasper flops onto his back, where he whimpers, his whole upper body tightening with shooting pain. Despite the unbearable cold, there's a fresh sheen of sweat along his brow. He's shivering, too. I move toward him, brushing Lana aside.

"What's this?" I ask him, and gently tap the bandage wrapped around his middle.

He appears to be in too much pain to reply, however.

"The men we picked up," Lana says. "Quentin and… Allen. They did this to him. Apparently they were looking for him when we picked them up. We just so happened to come here, bringing them straight to him…"

"Oh, God…" Jasper moans.

"I'm going to take a look," I say. "Is that all right with you, Jasper?"

Once more Jasper doesn't reply. Speechless with agony. I delicately grab the bandage and peel it away from his body, sticky with blood, revealing the wound underneath. The sight of it makes *me* ache—deeply bruised on the outer edges, swollen and inflamed in the middle. Still leaking, too

—blood and possibly other fluids besides. It's so awful to see, I have to resist clenching my own jaw.

"It's infected," I say. "That's why you're feverish."

"Are you a nurse, too?" Jasper asks.

I furrow my brow confusedly. "No, I'm not a nurse. Just a mother. What do you mean, *too*?"

Jasper lets out a shuddery breath, turning his head to the side.

"That woman... she used to be a nurse. Or a... a field medic, she said. She stitched me up."

I've still got Jasper's bandages pinched between my fingers, the wound on full display.

"I'm afraid she did no such thing, Jasper."

He looks at me again through downturned eyes. "Huh?"

"As far as I can tell... nothing's been done to treat this wound. It isn't cleaned. There aren't any stitches." I turn to Lana, whose face has gone even paler than usual at the sight of Jasper's gunshot. "He needs medical attention as soon as possible or he could die."

MISSY

*I*n the midst of my dread, as I stand outside their barricaded motel room door I try to consider my options, most of them reckless, many of them borderline insane. I grimace at the pain that flares through my shoulder where Jasper stabbed me, as well as the burning across my palm where he sliced me. I want to cry but I know I've done too much of that already.

I consider shooting aimlessly through their window. A desperate measure. I don't even know how many bullets I have left. One might assume that I should own a gun of my own, running a motel alone like I do, but I don't. Never have.

I consider setting fire to the whole place. Now *that* would be reckless. And insane. But then I could watch them scatter like roaches, pick them off as they come.

I figure I'm screwed no matter what I do. The mess has exceeded my ability to contain it. Too many graves to dig. Too many loose ends. For every soul that goes missing, there's no telling how many more will come looking. My only possible recourse is to ensure they don't leave this place, and that no trace of them is left when I'm through. They need to disappear. That means their bodies, their belongings, their vehicles, all gone—or at the very least, miles from this place, with nothing to tie them to me. The young woman did use her credit card to pay for their room, which is a problem, but not entirely damning. She also mentioned she has no cell service. Hopefully that's still the case. That's the only thing I've got going for me at this point. I can't have them contacting the authorities.

Deciding not to waste my remaining ammunition on a Hail Mary, I return to the truck. The keys are still sticking out of the door. I put them in my pocket. Jasper's bag of money lies forgotten in the snow, and a short distance from the bag I spot the kitchen knife I dropped—the one Jasper cruelly plunged into me. I grab that. I take it to their car still parked in front of Room 16 and stick both passenger-side tires to flatten them. I consider doing the same to the truck but ultimately decide against it. If by some miracle I manage to exterminate these people, I'll eventually need to move the truck in order to hide it. The same could be said for their sedan, of course, but they've left me no choice in that regard. I can't have them escaping while my back is turned.

When I peer toward their room again, the light in the window has gone dark. They're plotting, of course. *Scheming.*

I grab the bag of money and take it inside with me. I toss it back onto the kitchen table, then shut the sliding door and lock it again. I leave the wooden rod out of the track in case I need to make a quick exit. I toss the bloody knife—*my blood!*—into the kitchen sink. My shoulder truly aches. Nigh unbearable. I'm still in disbelief that Jasper could do such a thing, after everything I've done for him...

Disappointing. Always.

It isn't just him. It isn't just *them.* It's *all* so disappointing. All of it. Everything. As I study the gun in my hand, I'm hit with a spontaneous sensation I can't readily describe. It's a loathsome feeling. Despair, yet detached. It occurs to me how meaningless this is, like I'm scratching and clawing my way up a cliff for nothing.

What do I do, Geoffrey?

I want to burst into tears. But again, I don't. I can't. Instead I hurry into the lobby and ensure the door is properly locked. I double-check the motel's communication systems just for my own compulsive peace of mind and confirm everything is still disconnected—and has been since I first lugged Jasper into the guest bedroom upstairs. It was the first precaution I took as the night began unfolding.

I turn off the light in the kitchen. In the resulting darkness, I peer out the sliding glass door, where I can barely see a sliver of Room 7 beyond the truck that obscures most of my view. The wind has started kicking up again, coming in constant waves. The snow itself thins and thickens from the sky at an equally inconsistent rate. At this point I hope it never stops. I'm safe in here. I have everything I need, including my own vehicle parked within the safety of my garage. Unless an elderly woman and a dying man are willing to brave the storm, there's nowhere for them to go. They're stuck until I decide how I'm to deal with them.

It's the other one that concerns me. The girl. She's much

too clever for her own good. She's physically capable as well. More capable than I am in my current condition. But so long as I'm the only one with a firearm, I think I can keep her in check easily enough.

It's only a matter of waiting for them to slip.

LANA

I look between my grandma and the dying man on the motel bed.

"What should we do?"

"Well, first we should turn off these lights," my grandma says.

She does exactly this, dropping us into near pitch-black darkness. Only the faintest glow creeps in from around the window curtains as she peeks through them, surveying the parking lot.

"She's... gathering things from around the truck, I think."

"I dropped my bag," Jasper says. "It's got my wallet and my... money..."

I'm glad the lights are off, or else the others might see me fidgeting nervously as he says this.

"Money?" I say.

"...the money that got me into this mess."

I want to tell my grandma *'I told you so'*, but I hold my tongue. That she couldn't fathom Jason and Carl—or

Quentin and Allen—being criminals is so like her. Somehow she predicts my failings so well, but is so quick to give complete strangers the benefit of the doubt. I just wish she'd reserve some of her blind optimism for me, too. Oh well. Now is hardly the time for angst.

"She's just gone back inside," my grandma says, still scouting through the window. She lets go of the curtain, then turns to us and says, "What's wrong with her, exactly?"

"She's crazy," Jasper says. "She wanted to keep me here, and…"

He can't finish the thought, apparently, overcome with his aches and pains.

"We should leave," I say. "Now. While we can."

I gaze in Jasper's direction. I can only vaguely see his shape in the dark, on the bed. All I know is that I really don't want to spend the night with *another* dead body in this stinking motel.

"We need an actual plan," my grandma says. "She's got a gun, and she's obviously deranged…"

"The longer it takes us to think up a plan, the longer she has to come up with one of her own."

"We don't want to be hasty."

"We need to be hasty. We need to get out of here as soon as possible. Before he dies, like you said."

Jasper groans. "I really wish you'd stop saying that…"

"So what are you suggesting, Lana?"

I have to take a beat to think it over. The bare minimum.

"I'll get the car. I'll swing by outside and the two of you climb in. Jasper, can you walk at all?"

"I… can climb into a car…"

Just listening to him struggle to speak makes me feel similarly weak.

"Okay. I'm going, then."

"Wait," my grandma says.

"For what?"

"I don't know," she says, frustration flooding her voice. "I just don't want you running out there and getting yourself killed."

"I won't get myself killed," I say with as much confidence as I can muster, despite not believing a word I'm saying. "She's gone inside. She's probably tending to her wounds right now..."

"Wounds? What wounds?"

"I stabbed her," Jasper says, his pained voice laced with an air of pride.

"Whatever she's doing, she's busy for the time being," I say.

"Or maybe she's just waiting for us to make one wrong move," my grandma says. "If you go out there..."

"If I *don't* go out there, and we just sit here all night..."

Then Jasper will die, I think but don't say, as per his request.

"Okay," my grandma relents. "Just... watch that house like your life depends on it. And if she comes after you, forget about us. Okay? Just go get help. We'll be all right."

"I'll be quick."

I grab my car keys. I drag the dresser away from the door, just enough to open it. My heart is chugging. I just have to do it before I give myself a chance to realize how dangerous this really is, before I can second guess myself, before I get cold feet...

"Be ready," I tell them as I pull the door open and slip outside.

I jog through the snow toward my car, glancing intermittently at the motel manager's home. The windows are all dark now. I just know she's there somewhere, watching. My grandma was probably right. In a moment she'll emerge. In a moment it will be too late for me.

I practically throw myself upon my car as I jam the key into the door and unlock it. I climb behind the wheel, stick the keys into the ignition, and twist it to life. The engine rumbles pleasantly. I throw the car into REVERSE. In my rearview mirror, the red taillights glow against the falling snow.

Then the dashboard chirps at me—a warning.

The low tire pressure light is on.

What the hell?

Sometimes the warning light comes on when the temperature fluctuates. I'm not entirely sure how it could be *that,* however, considering we're well into winter now, but...

Forget it. I ignore the warning light, peering into the rearview mirror as I ease my foot onto the gas.

That's when I see her.

She approaches from the house, from the sliding glass door, just like my grandma feared she would. She's just a shadow, but I see the movement of her legs swishing in my direction, the movement of her arms as she lifts the object held in her hands. I already know what *that* is.

"Shit."

I gas it. The car lurches backward. The woman appears in my taillights, her gun aimed and ready to shoot. The car bumps and wobbles in a strange way, and without any help from the steering wheel I realize I'm reversing at an angle— a blessing in disguise as the woman attempts to shoot through the back windshield. Glass cracks. The bullet, wherever it's gone, misses me. I turn the steering wheel and she staggers out of the way as I let off the gas and the car continues to slide. I throw it into DRIVE. I floor it again. Some tires spin, some tires thump the ground like a rabbit's feet. The car turns in place, until finally the spinning tires find purchase on the asphalt beneath the snow and I'm off. I launch toward Room 7, but I know I can't pick the others up. I can't stop. I catch the briefest glimpse of my grandma in my headlights, peeking through the cracked door as I turn the wheel hand over hand. I turn instead alongside the motel, hurtling toward the exit, toward the road. Another gunshot goes off. Another pop. The window behind my seat shatters. I turn the wheel back and forth as the lopsided tires repeatedly try to spin me out.

"Come on, you stupid thing!"

She did this, obviously. Stuck my tires. Deflated them. Of course she'd think to do that. She's no dummy. She had to have known this vehicle was our only chance at leaving this place.

I can't go back for my grandma and Jasper. I *will* get myself killed if I try. But I can't just leave them here, either, can I? I have no choice. Maybe if I manage to drive this piece of shit into town, I can get help. Can they hold out long enough?

I let off the gas as I near the road. The red light from the roadside sign pours over me as I crank the wheel, turning slowly through the snow and ice. The car barely obeys.

Another gunshot. A tiny scream escapes me as it comes, as the bullet punches through the side of the car. I'm unharmed. I *think*. I step on the gas again, desperate to put distance between us, between this place and myself, between her gun and my head.

The car decides it's finished taking my orders. I start to slide. The back end of the vehicle swings out from behind me. I let off the gas again, apologizing profusely for being so presumptuous as to think I could tell the car what to do, as I continue turning the steering wheel in the other direction trying to correct course. I *do* correct course. Briefly. I follow the road a short distance before the car wobbles the other way, *spins* the other way. I struggle to thread the needle of this ice-covered road. I can't control it. I know I need to let off the gas completely, but in the back of my mind I know she's coming, she's chasing me with that damned gun. To stop is to be shot, to be killed, so I can't. But the car keeps fishtailing. The car keeps—

MISSY

*I*t's not the cold that has me trembling. It's everything else—the adrenaline surging through my veins, the terror in my heart as I watch her successfully pull the car onto the road and drive away. I aim and pull the trigger once more. I have no idea where the bullet goes. The car keeps moving, keeps *escaping.* I chase after her on shaky legs. Shaky everything. It's a miracle I can even grip the gun—that my quivering, frozen hands don't just release it into the snow.

My boots thump and scrape underneath me as I reach the road, out of breath, her taillights shrinking steadily into the black. I raise the gun once more. I actually try this time —lining its sights up between those red taillights—and pull the trigger once, twice, and then—

Those red orbs of light start to swivel back and forth. The car drifts towards the righthand edge of the road, until finally it tips into the ditch. Even through the wind I hear it. An audible *crash.* There's no chance she's got the traction to pull her way out of that. She's finished. I've got her.

My heart clamors as I jog toward the wreck. My eyes dart to either side of the car, examining the surrounding dark as snow swirls through the glow of the taillights. My sliced palm smarts as I grasp the gun in both hands, but I ignore it. I need all the grip I can get to stop myself from shaking. I look once over my shoulder, toward our little motel down the road which already looks so small in the dark, despite my not having walked very far.

The car ahead is still running. Still idling. Steam floats from its exhaust like a trail of cigarette smoke through the red. The tires aren't spinning. Not that I can see, or hear. The headlights are shining in a shallow, downward pool into the ditch.

Keeping a safe distance, I make my way around it, one foot over the other into the middle of the road. The driver's door is wide open. I advance, throwing caution to the howling wind.

No.

The seat is empty. The car is empty. She's not here. She's…

I spin, sweeping the gun across the shadows, my shoulder alight with fiery pain. I scour the empty fields. I eye the ground beside the car and discover her footprints. She's moved into the ditch itself, along the length of it. I peer in that direction but see nothing.

How far could she have gone? It's been mere seconds.

I follow the ditch, sniffing back a leaky nose, frozen to the bone even in my jacket. But it isn't long before I lose the footprints entirely. They simply vanish. I turn in place, keeping the gun up and at the ready. The icy wind bites at my cheeks. There's no sign of her. The footprints fade, or change course, or…

This is impossible!

I climb the slope of the ditch, back onto the road, drawing my gaze across the flurry. I peer toward the car, an island of light in the stormy void, the next island that of our motel in the distance. There's nothing out here. Nowhere for her to run. It's late enough that I doubt these roads will be seeing any more traffic tonight, so there's little chance she'll find help on foot.

Where the hell are you?

A lump forms in my throat. Helplessness. Hopelessness. Everything that could go wrong has gone wrong. I don't know what else to do. My eyes burn with tears that I refuse to let spill.

Where the hell are *you*, Geoffrey? Why aren't you here? Why aren't you here to tell me my next move? What do I do? Where do *I* go? I'm so lost. I'm so, so lost…

It's out of my control.

DARLENE

I stuff my feet into my boots. I don't bother with the laces. I pull my coat back on. It's cold as heck out there in my pajamas, but that's the least of my worries now.

"Jasper?" It's difficult to see him now with the lights off. "Can you stand?"

I find him in the dark, seated at the end of the bed. I put my arms around his shoulders and try to help him onto his feet with what little strength my brittle bones can provide him.

"Bear in mind... I'm not as strong as my grand-daughter..."

He groans as he stands against me. He trusts me a little *too* much, his weight just about knocking me over. We both stay standing, however. I help him to the door, which is still open just a crack. I pull it open enough to peer outside. Lana's already started the car, all its lights aglow. Now she's pulling out—

I gasp as another gunshot claps the night. I see the flash

of the barrel, the gun in her hands, the woman just a shadow until Lana's taillights illuminate her there in the middle of the parking lot. Lana's car slides. The woman nearly topples as she dances out of the way. Then Lana's hurtling forward again, driving straight toward us, except something's obviously wrong. Very, *very* wrong.

"Oh dear," is all I can say as Lana steers herself elsewhere, the tail end of her car swishing this way and that. Her tires thump and thwack in the snow as she goes, until she seems to straighten out some. Only for a moment. And then…

"Where's she going?" Jasper asks, as we each watch my granddaughter swerve her way to the road, leaving us behind. The motel manager follows after her, her skinny little legs jogging delicately across the ice in pursuit.

"She can't stop," I say.

Not unless she wants to get shot, anyway. There comes another pop of gunfire. I nearly choke on my own heart. I hold my breath, listening. A gust of wind sweeps a phantom of snow through the parking lot. Then I hear nothing at all. No more gunshots. Nothing.

"She's gone. She's gotten away."

I don't know this for a fact. I'm speaking hopefully. Perhaps in denial. Did that final gunshot do its job? I pray to every god in this universe that it didn't.

"Hold on a moment, Jasper," I say, and lean him against the dresser that's been dragged near the door.

"You can't go out there."

"I need to see. I need to make sure…"

I step outside. I shuffle through the snow into the parking lot, far enough that I have a view of the road.

Caught in the red glow of the motel sign, I see the manager standing out there, in the road, staring off into the distance. Did Lana escape? Is she driving away?

God, I hope so.

Then the manager sprints away, farther along the road, out of sight. I don't know what that could mean. Where could she possibly be going if Lana has already gotten away?

Something wasn't right with her car.

Winter sinks its teeth firmly into me. I hurry back to the room and shut the door behind me.

"What's going on?" Jasper says.

"My granddaughter seems to have gotten away, but…"

"But what?"

"I don't know. Her car was all over the place. It almost sounded like she was driving on flats. I just… I don't know."

"She'll get help," Jasper says. "If she gets away, then maybe…"

"I'm not sure she's gotten away just yet. I just watched the manager go running off down the road after her."

This has me fearing the absolute worst. If Lana couldn't control her car, it's possible she didn't actually get very far.

"Listen," Jasper says, then falters as he sucks in breath. His gunshot wound is still bothering him a great deal, clearly. "I can't be positive, but… there might be another gun in Quentin's truck. I never checked, but… usually there would be. Something in the glovebox, probably. Him and his guys rarely go anywhere without some extra… *assurances*."

"Unless that woman's already searched it," I say. "She'd be smart to, if she's up to... *whatever* you say she's up to."

I know he must have an entire story of his own—how he ended up in this predicament, what he's endured at the hands of that woman out there. I'm interested in hearing his story, but obviously now isn't the time.

"She's killed a lot of people," he says, and my blood runs cold. Colder than it already was. "She's dangerous."

"And I've never shot a gun in my life."

"I have," Jasper says.

"You're in no shape to be on your feet. More than you already are, I mean."

"I know. But it's our only shot at protecting ourselves."

Only shot. A funny choice of words.

"If she's distracted with your granddaughter, right now might be our best chance."

I know something must be done. Jasper and I are entirely too vulnerable in here. There's no way either of us are pushing that dresser back against the door. But even if we could, what then? Jasper will die. I'll spend the night alone while that woman bides her time, waiting for me to expire. That is, if Lana doesn't reach help. I don't know. There are just so many uncertainties.

"All right," I say. "I'll go check out the truck. Hopefully I've got time."

Hopefully Lana is all right. Hopefully she's leading that bat on a wild goose chase.

"I'll be back."

I step out into the cold once more. The bitter night stings my cheeks, my hands. It seeps through my pajama bottoms and into my legs, into my very bones as I make haste across the parking lot toward the truck. I cast a nervous glance toward the road along the way. I don't see her or anyone else.

I try the driver's door and it opens. It's a bit of a step. I'm not even sure I can pull myself inside without losing my grasp and falling. I grab the steering wheel and the frame of the door, pulling myself up as I stomp my boot onto the ledge under the door. The steering wheel turns slightly in my grasp. Groaning, I haul myself up and into the driver's seat with a dramatic sigh.

"Oh my goodness," I say, already exhausted.

I lean into the passenger seat and fumble with the glovebox. I pop it open. A light comes on from inside, which lets me see some paper documents that are stored in there, as well as some boxes of...

Bullets.

There are boxes of bullets, but no gun.

Now what?

I dread climbing down from the truck, but obviously I must do it. I hold onto the open door as I return my feet to the ledge, and delicately lower myself back down. My first boot crunches into the snow, followed by the other. I sigh another breath of relief and shut the truck door.

All for nothing, unfortunately.

I start to leave back to the motel room when something catches my eye. That's when I notice the rear door of the house. A sliding glass door.

It's standing wide open.

LANA

*T*he impact jostles me forward. The deploying airbag punches me right back. My head rocks off the headrest. Then everything stops. My face is half-numb, half-chafed. The air smells burnt.

It takes me back in an instant. That smell.

I'm in the car with her again.

With mom. *Mommy.*

Everything is quiet and still after the crash. Except for her. Mom isn't quiet or still. She's shaking in her seat and there's foam rolling out of her mouth. But it's not the crash that's done it. No, that started before the crash. It's the medicine she takes. That's what she calls it, anyway. Her medicine. She said we shouldn't really be driving but we've got places to be. Except this is the only place she gets us—crashed into a median, her eyes rolled back, her heart beating itself into oblivion.

The sounds of my own girlish screams fill my ears as I remember her like that, in her final moments.

And then blood drips into my eye.

My left eye is blurry and red with it. Dazed, I swab the blood away and suddenly remember where I am. It's dark and cold except for the blood dripping down my forehead, where I've been grazed by a bullet, it seems. I hadn't noticed until now. I guess the motel manager is a better shot than I thought.

I sit forward in my seat. I look about myself, at the deflating airbag, out the window ahead, where the head-lights are darkened against the snow-filled ditch. I turn in my seat, in the direction of the motel, and I see her coming. *Still coming.* Like the goddamn Terminator. She's dark and small against the red glow of 'The 11th Hour Motel' sign, but she's steadily making her way up the road after me. I need to move.

I wipe more blood away as I feel it starting to drip into my eye again. I came within inches of death and didn't even know it.

Move already.

I push my door open, stagger out into the snow. I crouch, staying low as I abandon the car, scurrying into the ditch itself alongside the road, moving as quickly as I can. The car's light should blind her to the darkness beyond it, at least. The darkness I'm in. For a short time.

Then I remember what I'm running through—what I'm leaving behind.

I look over my shoulder once and see her arriving at the scene, stepping around the back of my car. Her attention is on the car itself as she approaches the open door. I have a literal second before she realizes I'm gone, and she'll know exactly *where* I've gone the instant she looks at the tracks I've left in the snow.

Somehow I need to sever the string of footprints I'm—

My foot catches on something in the ditch. A deep rut underneath the snow. I pitch forward, hit the ground hard. A gasp escapes me, along with most of the air in my lungs. I wheeze. I can't help it. Did she hear that? I push myself onto my hands and knees as another warm droplet of blood slips into my eye. I crawl on all fours, half-blinded. I try to swipe the blood away to no avail.

Behind me, her footsteps scuff to a stop and I freeze.

I drop back down, lying as flat as I possibly can in the snow. She caught up fast. Unexpectedly close. I discreetly pull the hood of my coat over my head. It's a white coat. Maybe I'll blend in. I pray that I will. My sweatpants are a light gray. Maybe they'll do the trick, too. Or maybe they won't. Maybe I stick out like a sore thumb, lying flat on my face waiting for a bullet through my back.

I still haven't caught the breath I've lost, but I hold what little I have all the same.

Her boots thump closer. She's so close I hear her panting. I tense, flexing my every sore muscle, anticipating a gunshot that never comes.

Instead she climbs out of the ditch and onto the road. She paces about. I hear her muttering to herself, under the sound of the wind and flecking snow.

"Oh god, oh god… please, no… no, no, no…"

I flinch where I lay as she screams. *Shrieks.* An animal sound. Utter frustration. Aggravation. A pitiful, wet sob escapes her. I don't think she's looking for me anymore so much as she's having a full-blown tantrum in the middle of the road.

My curiosity gets the better of me again. I turn my head

ever so slightly within the shelter of my hood, and lift my head just enough to take a peek toward the road beside me. She turns in useless circles there, retracing her steps and turning back, hitching sobs escaping her all the while. She pushes her hand through her sandy hair, her gun held loosely at her side. I can vaguely see the contours of her face, pinched with emotion. She erupts with another terrible scream and I hide myself away again, lowering my head back against the icy ground—a turtle retreating back into its shell.

This goes on for a minute or more. I'm certain she's going to notice me at some point.

Then her footsteps move away. The sound of her anguish fades with distance.

Somehow, I've survived.

DARLENE

I know Jasper is waiting for me. I know this is dangerous, what I'm doing. But I feel I must do *something*. I can't go back empty-handed. I can't just hide the rest of the night away.

The open door looks like an opportunity. It looks like something I'm meant to take advantage of, and so I do.

I step inside the house, into what appears to be a dark kitchen. I leave the door open behind me, in case I need to quickly escape outside again.

There's a hallway across the kitchen leading toward the front of the house, where a light is still on. A dim light, like from a lamp. Before venturing that way, however, I investigate the kitchen table where a duffel bag has been placed. I peek inside and find so much money I nearly gasp. This must be the money Jasper mentioned—the money that got him into all this trouble, like he said. Sounds to me like it was never his to begin with. *That's* the trouble. Is greed alone responsible for all this tragedy tonight? I suppose it should come as no surprise to me, but I can still scarcely believe it.

Ignoring the money, I see no sign of the keys to the truck outside, which was what I privately hoped to find when I entered through the open door. Perhaps I'll find them elsewhere. The only problem is I don't know how much time I have left before the manager returns.

I notice a second offshoot to my left, a short little hallway that looks as though it leads nowhere. But no, there is a door there, at its end. I think I have an idea where that might lead. I make my way there, and open the door to pitch black darkness and a noticeable breath of cold. I flip the light switch along the wall inside and reveal the garage, along with the full-size SUV parked inside it. That must be the manager's vehicle. Again, however, it doesn't do me any good without keys.

I return to the kitchen, to the longer hallway that leads toward the front of the house. There I discover a long counter that's been installed with space to stand behind it, like a check-in desk you'd find in a regular motel lobby. I search all over the desk, behind it, and see no sign of car keys. I also try the corded phone on the wall but it's not working.

"Darn it, anyway."

I stand at the foot of the stairs. Could there be anything up there? I feel as though I've used up all the time I have. To venture upstairs would be suicide, I'm certain.

I startle as something bumps against the front door. I turn to face it. The doorknob jiggles. Then, after a brief pause, it jiggles again as someone slides their key inside.

MISSY

*T*here's nothing I can do about it anymore. She's escaped. The loose thread has truly gotten away from me now. Everything will unravel. It's a matter of *when*, not *if*.

My thoughts are in so many pieces, I can't think straight. It *hurts* to think. My head is pounding. I'm not sure what my next move should even be at this point, with my undoing so close. So…

Inevitable.

Another whimper squeaks out of me. I can't help myself. I'm weak, Geoffrey. I've always been weak. You knew that better than anyone. Without you, I'm just… *nothing*, really. Isn't that right?

I start back to the motel, but not before I snatch the keys from the crashed sedan. Wherever she is, wherever she's run off to, or wherever she's hiding, she'll be stranded unless she wants to come back for these, or hike miles through the bitter cold. I'll leave that up to her. I hope she freezes to death, personally.

I trample my way back home, huddling into myself against the blowing wind the whole way there. I feel as though the wind has caught the loose ends trailing off of me, pulling them long and ribboning into the dark as I dwindle into less and less. Each step back to our motel, I feel a little emptier. Sunken. Will I even make it back? Or will there be nothing left of me by then? I fear the storm will carry me away forever.

But nothing can ever be so easy. I make it back to the motel in one piece. Without thinking, I try to let myself in before remembering that I've locked the entrance. I fish my keys out of my pocket, cycle through them until I find the one I need, unlock the door, step into the cozily lit lobby, and shut the door behind me.

Then I just stand in place for a time.

Is this really it? Is this what my life has been leading up to? Everything I've worked so hard for? Everything I've overcome? Am I simply meant to wait for fate to have its way with me? My inevitable arrest is on the horizon. There's nothing I can do to escape it, I think. Although, I might have hours to spare until then. *Hours.* The thought alone is painful. The idea of waiting. I'm not sure I can endure it.

It's over, Missy. It's really, truly, honestly over.

Coals burn behind my eyes. I choke on the same lump in my throat.

It's not easy being a widow. I feel as though I've been trapped under the rubble of some terrible misunderstanding. No one will understand the truth. *My* truth. *Our* truth.

I swipe tears from my eyes and, as my mind is not cooperating, I allow my heart to guide me instead. I find myself moving into the dark hallway, into the living room where my movie—*that stupid, stupid movie*—has now been paused for so long that the DVD player's screensaver is bouncing around on my television's dimmed screen. I move past the television, to the shelf on the wall behind it, where I take down one of several framed photographs. It's my favorite photograph. I take a seat in my chair, where I set the gun in my lap so that I can hold the photograph in both hands.

It's you. It's a picture of you, taken only a few years before you passed. Handsome as ever. My eyes are truly on fire now, brimming with tears I have to blink back. Your visage shimmers. My face contorts and I can't stop it. I want to bawl but the *ball* in my throat won't let anything by. My tears drip onto the glass of the frame and for a moment I fantasize that the power of love and sorrow can bring you back to me, that my tears on your photograph might magically make you materialize as you are in the picture. If only I'd thought to cry upon it sooner!

But no. Instead, my tears make a mess of the dust that's gathered on the glass, creating dirty little splotches in the fine, gray film.

I've spent so many years yearning, wishing for the impossible. I'll never have you back. Not in this life. I've always known that, of course. But something about my impending ruin makes it clearer than ever before—all the time I've wasted yearning for the impossible. You are gone and will stay gone, so long as I'm here.

Which gets me thinking...

Perhaps there is another way.

I set your photograph aside, between my leg and the arm of the chair. I pick up the gun once more. I cradle it in both hands. It's a heavy little thing. So small and yet capable of something so... *big*. Or maybe it's not. Maybe it's *not* so big. It only feels big from here. Perhaps what actually follows puts it all into perspective, makes it smaller. I only have to do it. Like ripping off a Band-Aid.

For all I know, you've been waiting for this moment. Waiting for *me*. Maybe you wish I'd done it sooner. I just had no way of knowing.

I'm beginning to wish I'd done it sooner, too.

I turn the gun toward myself, place its cold barrel into my mouth, between my teeth. It tastes like you'd expect.

And then the shadows gasp.

I open my eyes wide as I hear it—a voice in the dark. I take the gun from my mouth and turn to those whispering shadows beside me, the darkness that clings to the wall beside the doorway where I entered from the hall. There's a shape there, someone concealed, someone watching me all the while. I stand abruptly from the chair. Your photograph tumbles to the floor in the process. I point the gun at the waiting phantom.

"Who's there?"

The shape doesn't move at first. Then it steps forward into the soft light coming through the doorway and I see it's the old woman from Room 7. Her hands are raised in surrender. Truce. I keep the gun aimed exactly as it is.

"Oh. It's *you*."

"Darlene," she replies. "My name's Darlene."

"I don't care what your name is."

Miraculously, my anxiety from before is gone. I've never felt so calm in my life. It's the strangest thing—stepping so close to the precipice of *nothing* has rendered me uncaring. I no longer feel the urgency of my situation. What's done is done, it is what it is, so on and so forth. My hands don't even tremble anymore.

"This is all your fault," I tell the old woman. "If not for you and your granddaughter… showing up with those men, those *criminals*… none of this would have happened. Everything would be like it's supposed to be. Like it should have been."

"Did you lose someone?" she asks, ignoring what I've said. She nods toward something behind me. I'm not sure what she means. "Someone dear to you?"

I realize she's referring to your photograph, now on the ground beside my feet. Her mention of it, of *you*, instills me with so much *annoyance* I can hardly stand it.

"That's none of your business…"

"I lost someone, too," she says, even though I haven't asked. "It's not easy. I know."

I tell myself I couldn't care less about her loss or what she has to say about mine, and yet my heart betrays me. Those burning coals ignite once again behind my eyes. I blink back more tears. I want to pull the trigger so badly. I want to shut her up, make her go away so that I can carry on with my business. I know she's stalling. I know she's only speaking to me to save herself. So why can't I pull the damn trigger? Why does my head feel so swollen with tears? Why is my sorrow-slurred tongue wagging?

"I lost my husband," I tell her. I'm not sure why I'm telling her. Perhaps it's simply that nobody has ever asked me before.

"When did you lose him?"

None of your damned business, I think but do not say.

I have to think about it. Why do I have to think about it? It's not like I've forgotten.

"Years ago. Years and years. He was... in a terrible accident."

I have to clear my throat as the lump forms yet again. I feel as if my whole head is fit to burst from the pressure. The old woman's shadowy form blurs in my vision.

"He was badly burned. Most of his body. I cared for him until the very end. We only had each other, and... now I have no one."

"Oh," the old woman says, and her response strikes me as bizarre. *Oh?* Is that all you have to say? Really? *Oh?* "I'm so sorry to hear that."

"No you're not," I snap.

An enormous heat rises up in me, unexpected. My annoyance deepens into something else. Why have I told this woman a single thing about my life? About you? She doesn't care about me. She doesn't appreciate what I've shared with her. Of course not. Nobody really cares.

"You don't give a shit about me. You don't give a shit about *anyone.* You and that *thief* you call your granddaughter. I should end your miserable life right now like I ended hers."

It's a lie, but it feels so good. Even in the dark, and through the watery shimmer of my tears, I can see the change in the old woman as she stiffens where she stands, the vague details of her face drawing tighter than they've probably been in years.

"You didn't," she says.

"You bet I did. And she deserved it. You both do, after everything you've put me through tonight."

The gun in my hand has lowered over the last minute or so, as I've let my guard down during all of this useless chatter. But now I remember myself. I tighten my grip on the weapon in my hands. I raise it again, centered on the old woman, my trigger finger curled.

"No," the old woman says, shaking her head. "No, you don't get to play the victim. You're no victim. You're just another senseless criminal."

"And you're just another halfwit who doesn't know when to shut their mouth," I retort, my finger flexing across the trigger.

"You're a terrible liar, too," she goes on. I can scarcely believe she'd be so bold in her current predicament. "Your husband didn't really die like you say, did he?"

Her question stuns me so suddenly that I momentarily forget the gun in my hands, as well as the tears in my eyes.

"Excuse me? You don't know the first thing about me..."

"You're no Juliette Binoche, I know that much."

I open my mouth to reply but words fail me. Did I hear that right? Did she really just say what I think she said?

"*The English Patient* is a perfectly tragic story, but that's all it is. A story. And it isn't yours. I'm guessing you killed your husband like all the others. Am I right?"

"What..." I'm at a loss. How could she possibly know any of this? How could she know anything about me, or my life? Then I remember Jasper. He might have told her something. Where is he now, I wonder?

"Am I right?" she repeats. "Did you kill your husband?"

It's like she wants to rile me up. It's like she's got a

death wish, like she saw me with the gun in my mouth and decided she wants her turn first.

"What was his crime, I wonder?" she says. "He cheat on you? That was it, wasn't it? I can tell by the look on your face. But the joke was on him, huh. He had no idea he was married to a different kind of monster…"

"Be quiet," I say, trying my absolute hardest to regain control of this conversation, to ensure I get the final say, the last laugh. "Maybe I am a monster. But he's *nothing* now. Nothing but a pile of bones in a field of no-good liars… where you'll soon be buried, too."

I pull the trigger.

JASPER

*A*s soon as the old woman steps outside, I manage to hobble my way to the window and lean there instead, peering out into the dark where I watch as she disappears around the other side of the truck.

Then minutes go by. She never reappears.

Come on, lady.

Obviously something's wrong. Somehow I knew something would happen. Despite my warning, she has no idea what she's truly dealing with—or what she's up against.

Has the manager returned? Intervened? Am I all alone now, simply waiting for the worst to come?

I'm so exhausted, the only thing stopping me from dumping myself onto the motel bed and letting go for good is the thought of *her.* Jennifer is waiting for me. Looking for me. Wondering where I've vanished to…

"Come on," I whisper, as I watch those shadows along the back of the house, begging the old woman to reappear, to come back already, keys in hand.

But it's been too long. More than enough time for the manager to come back, I think.

If I stay here, I'm dead. If I go out there, I'm probably dead.

Probably isn't a guarantee, at least.

"Fuck me," I mutter as I shuffle my way to the door once again.

I pull it open. The cold whirls around my naked body. I stumble out onto the walkway and my toes are instantly chilled, the bottoms of my feet burned by cold fire. I hurry as fast as I can. My guts continue to ache and squirm inside me, but the overwhelming pain has subsided some— another sign of imminent death, maybe? By the time I reach the truck, I can hardly feel my feet anymore. My body shivers uncontrollably. There's no sign of the old woman out here. The sliding glass door is open. She must have gone inside. Maybe in search of the truck keys? Was she at least able to check inside the truck, I wonder? Did she find a gun? I fucking hope so.

I stumble my way into the sliding glass doorway and that's when I hear them.

Two voices. Two women.

"Did you kill your husband?"

The old woman's voice. She's still alive. And the manager *has* returned. They're in the next room, but it's so dark that I can't see anything from the doorway. I'm afraid to move, that I'll trip over myself and make too much noise.

"What was his crime, I wonder? He cheat on you? That was it, wasn't it? I can tell by the look on your face. But the joke was on him, huh. He had no idea he was married to a different kind of monster..."

On quivering legs, I slip into the house. I tiptoe to the table, toward the doorway beyond it that leads into the living room from the kitchen. My breaths are labored, shuddering. I have to fight to stay quiet without holding my breath altogether. I move into the living room doorway and finally see them—the manager with her back to me, her gun aimed at the old woman near the opposite doorway that leads into the hall. The manager is speaking now, rattling off some villainous babble, but I don't have time to listen. The old woman doesn't have time for me to listen, either. I approach on my numb, prickling feet. I open my arms as I go, as if I'm planning to give the motel manager a warm hug from behind.

"...*where you'll soon be buried, too...*"

I throw myself around her as the gun goes off. The bullet hits something, but it's not me and it's not the old woman and that's all that matters. I wrap my arms tightly around her, grabbing hold of her arms in kind, and jerk the gun toward the lifeless shadows where she pulls the trigger a second time, another harmless shot. She growls as we stumble in place. I step on something and it cracks under my heel. Broken wood and glass. A framed photograph. I pull the manager backward and we bump against the television set. It falls off its stand and clatters to the floor face-down beside us.

Suddenly the old woman is here. It's hard to tell what she's doing as we stumble about, but I hear a distinct *whap, whap, whap* as she strikes the manager in the dark. With her arms entangled in mine, the manager kicks the old woman, sends her sprawling to the floor, sends *us* staggering backward against the wall where I'm crushed in between. She elbows me right in the stomach. My mouth screams, my belly ignites. My grip around her slackens and she escapes me. She stumbles forth, catches herself against her chair. Then she pivots to face me, brandishing the gun across the shadows likewise.

"No!" the old woman shouts as the subsequent gunshot drowns her out.

This bullet hits something, too.

My chest blooms with fire. I grab hold of it. My chest. The fire. It soaks my hand in an instant. I'm already resting against the wall, which is convenient as what little strength I have left leaves my body, leaves me slumped and sliding down the wall to the floor. She steps closer. The gun in her hand vibrates uncontrollably, so she steadies it against my forehead and pulls the trigger again.

This time the gun clicks empty—not that she needs another bullet to finish me off. I think the one in my chest will do. She drops the empty gun to the floor, nothing more than a hunk of metal now. She crouches before me. She cocks her head, staring me in the eye with a bewildering look I can't even begin to translate. She almost looks sorry, like she's just realized she's made a terrible mistake.

"You stupid, *stupid*…"

She doesn't finish the thought. The old woman stirs across the room, trying to pick herself up off the floor, reminding the manager that her work isn't done yet. She briskly stands and darts after her. The old woman cries out. I can't see them, but there's a struggle. Strained grunts and heavy panting.

There's nothing I can do to help. Not her. Not myself.

My luck is finally running out in a steady stream down my chest.

LANA

Once I'm certain she's left—and when the cold becomes too unbearable to lay in any longer—I stand up from the ditch. My face still hurts, like someone's punched me square in the nose. My blood has stopped trickling into my eye, at least. Or rather, the cold has since frozen my blood in place, thick and frosted down my forehead.

I climb out of the ditch and onto the road. There's still no sign of life or rescue in the distance. Not a single pair of headlights. I suppose it's late and the roads are still shit, but you'd think *someone* would come. Anyone.

It's a strange feeling to have escaped, but not yet be saved.

Do I hike to the nearest town and hope I don't freeze to death before I get there? Or do I go back to the motel, with the moderate advantage of being unaccounted for, whatever good that will do me?

My grandma can't fight that crazy bitch on her own.

And that man, Jasper, is half dead already so he won't be much help to her, either, I think.

I can't just leave her there.

And that's that.

I stop by my car first. She's already taken the keys, not that I could drive it anywhere anyhow, slanted into the ditch like it is. I pop the trunk. From the trunk I pull out the silver tire iron I keep—just an ordinary L-shaped one. Besides a gun of my own, it's as good a weapon as I could hope for.

Am I really going back?

Yes. I could never live with myself if I left my grandma alone and the worst should happen. Even though I've already technically left her there. But there was nothing I could do then. I couldn't stop.

And it was my idea to pull that stupid stunt in the first place.

What would have happened, I wonder, if I'd never attempted to escape in the car? We'd still be sitting in that motel room, I suppose, waiting for the manager to make her next move while Jasper dies of infection. To be brutally honest, I would have been fine with him dying if it meant my grandma and I were safe. But she's better than I am. She didn't want to wait around and watch him die, either.

So I did what I thought I needed to do.

These are the thoughts I dwell on as I make the journey back down the road toward that batshit place. It waits in the dark like a bad omen.

The 11th Hour Motel.

We should have kept driving. But of course hindsight, *yada yada yada,* and all the rest…

I wrinkle my nose and immediately wince from the

pain. I think it might be broken. It would explain the taste of blood in the back of my throat. Did the airbag really do that?

I approach the motel on reluctant feet. I peer along the length of it, where Room 7 sits in the rear crook of the parking lot. Everything looks as it did when I drove off. My grandma and Jasper are probably still holed up inside, with nothing to—

The sound of gunshots startles me. Two of them, coming from the house, I think. Shit.

I run to the entrance, gripping the tire iron tight as I grab hold of the doorknob. That's when a third gunshot rings out. My stomach clenches. I freeze.

They say your life flashes before your eyes when you die, but in this moment it's my grandma's life that flashes before mine—early-riser breakfasts together in the morning, daytime television in the afternoon, bedtime stories at night, more laughter condensed in singular days than I'd experienced in the first nine years of my life.

I pull the door open. The warmth from inside touches my numb face and body like a welcome embrace but I can't enjoy it. I move without thinking. Autopilot. I take one step after another, gliding swiftly toward the only sounds I can hear—murmurs from down the hall. I fully expect to stare down the barrel of a gun when I turn the corner, to have my candles blown out once and for all. Instead I find all their bodies on the floor. My grandma is on her back, the manager straddling her.

Her hands are around my grandma's throat.

By the time she looks up to see me, the tire iron is already in full swing. I catch her by the side of the face, can practically feel her cheekbone shatter under the weight of my weapon as the strike reverberates into my hands, my wrists.

The cavewoman noise that escapes me is new.

The motel manager falls aside, and the whine that floats from her gaping mouth triggers something in me. It's not sympathy. It's quite the opposite—the urge a canine must feel when it gives its squealing prey a violent thrashing.

I step over my grandma—she's moving, she's clasping her throat, she's gasping, she's *alive*—and I bring the tire iron over my head as the manager squirms onto her back, one palm raised in a gesture that's lost in translation as I hit her again. I club her right between the eyes. She drops like an empty sock puppet.

Her eyes are open but they're empty.

That's when I come back to myself.

I drop the tire iron to the floor. Then I drop to my knees beside my grandma as she chokes and wheezes.

"Grandma." I delicately put my hands on her shoulders. "Are you okay? Can you breathe?"

She can't speak over all the coughing, but she nods her head in reply.

"Here, let's get you up…"

She bats my hands away, sitting up on her own. She remains seated on the floor, however, as she points a shaking finger across the room.

That's when I see him.

JASPER

I can't believe how worried I was before, about dying. That wasn't dying. *This* is dying. The difference is night and day. Life and death. I can actually feel it happening, and I'm... not as scared as I thought I'd be. It's weird. I actually feel pretty good. I feel comfortable. The pain is gone—in my stomach and in my heart.

Unfortunately the old woman is dying, too, though. I wish I could help her. Failing that, I wish I could tell her it's not so bad, dying. It's cozier than you'd think. Like having the perfect buzz. I'm floating but I'm still. I'm loose but I'm solid.

Then again, I'm not staring my killer in the face like she is.

I take a deep breath just as someone else enters the room. The younger one. I'm not sure I caught her name, but she swings like Ted Williams. Even in my delirious state I startle at the suddenness of the sound. A meaty *thwack*. Then the motel manager is on the floor, and it's not long before another swing soon follows. She doesn't get up from the second one. I don't think she ever will, either. There and gone in seconds, with hardly a moment to understand the difference.

She doesn't get to enjoy death like I do.

The old woman is alive. She's catching her breath while I'm still dying.

Then she comes over to me. The younger one. She crouches down beside me and peers into my eyes with hers all afraid and panicked, searching for something she can do to help, but I think we both know there isn't anything she can do for me.

Well, no, that's not entirely true.

I try to speak. My tongue is an untamed beast that resists my commands. I have to really fight for them, the words, but I know if there's one last thing worth fighting for in this life, it's this.

A sound comes out of my mouth, but it's not at all what I'm trying to say. Luckily it's enough to let the young woman know I'm trying to tell her something. She leans in closer to hear.

"Jennifer," I finally manage to spit out.

The young woman pulls away slightly, looking deeply into my eyes. She shakes her head.

"No," she says. "I'm Lana."

Lana. That's a lovely name. Almost as lovely as Jennifer.

Now it's my turn to shake my head.

"No," I say. She leans in close again because my voice is barely more than a whisper. "The money... take it to her. Please."

She regards me like I'm talking crazy, like I'm not making any sense, which is frustrating. I don't know how else to say it. I think I'm being pretty clear. She shakes her head again.

"We're gonna get you out of here," she says, and begins looking around herself, peering into the kitchen, and I'm struck with an intense fear that she's going to walk away and leave me here in search of some hopeless attempt to save me. I know my time is up. I think I might only have seconds left, a minute at most. So I reach out to her, slap a hand on her shoulder to stop her from going, to force her to focus on me, *please.*

"No," I repeat. "It's over." She looks like she wants to argue, so I shake my head again. "Please. Make sure... make sure it gets to her. To Jennifer. *Jennifer.* She's..." How do I say this? How do I explain succinctly with the few seconds I have left? "My phone. It's in the bag..." I gesture weakly toward the kitchen. "The money..."

I can't describe the swell of relief I feel as the young woman—*Lana*—nods in understanding. It's the strongest relief I've ever felt, more relieving than death itself, like I can relax for the first time in my life. The final time.

I do just that. I relax. I lay my head back against the wall and take another long, deep breath into my lungs which can hardly hold air anymore. The young woman is saying something but I don't hear her. Or I don't listen. Instead I close my eyes and I think of Jennifer. I see her clear as day in my mind's eye, smiling over her shoulder at me in that coy way she does when she's being a tease. She's cradling something in her arms. No, not something, but some*one.* A beautiful baby girl. She smiles at me, too, and that smile is the most wonderful thing I've ever laid eyes on, I think.

Hello, Gloria.

LANA

*T*he guy is on his last breath. He leans his head back and closes his eyes. My eyes can't stop flitting downward to the gruesome wound in his chest, fresh blood pooling into his lap.

He wants me to get his phone.

I hurry into the kitchen where he pointed. His money bag has since been replaced on the table after he'd dropped it outside. I open it up and find a couple new items—a wallet and a phone, presumably his. I grab the phone. I bring it back into the living room and find him with a smile on his face.

"I have your phone." I grab his hand from his lap and try putting his phone into his palm, and notice how utterly limp he's become. I push against his shoulder. "Jasper."

It becomes clear to me that he's gone, even as the smile remains fixed to his mouth. Whatever he was thinking in his last moments must have been comforting. At first I'm not sure what to do. I tap the screen on his phone and I'm presented with a fingerprint reader. I take his hand, still warm to the touch, and press his thumb to the screen, unlocking it. He has the same cell service I do —zilch. I open his contacts, where I scroll to find *Jennifer*. Her oval picture stares back at me. She's very pretty, which makes sense. Jasper is—or was—very handsome himself.

"Oh, dear," my grandma says.

I stop what I'm doing for a moment and peer in her direction, where she stands over the motel manager's corpse. The look on my grandma's face fills me with guilt, but I shrug it aside and focus on Jasper's phone again. As I resume what I'm doing, my grandma hobbles up behind me.

"Oh, dear…"

"Yeah," I murmur, glancing fleetingly at Jasper's peaceful face. "He's gone…"

I take out my own phone and add Jennifer as a contact, for later. Then I place Jasper's phone into his hand, in his lap. I watch him for a long, long moment, my thoughts circling uselessly as my eyes wander over his face to the wound in his chest, to the bandage around his stomach.

"He saved my life," my grandma says. "And then so did you…"

I stand up and return into the kitchen, to the table where the bag of money sits. My grandma follows after me.

"The phones are disconnected," she says. "I tried the landline in the lobby and it wasn't working, either."

"Yeah. We'll just have to take ourselves into town."

"There's the truck out back, or the woman's SUV in the garage."

The thought of climbing into that woman's vehicle gives

me the heebie-jeebies. I don't want to touch anything else that belonged to her if I can help it.

"We'll take the truck."

Returning into the living room, I quickly search through the manager's jacket pockets until I find several sets of keys. One is obviously hers, with all the motel room spares. The other set is sparser and includes the key to the truck out back. I pocket those. Then my eyes happen upon the tire iron on the ground. Another wave of guilt flashes over me. Should I take that with me, too? I didn't murder anyone in cold blood, I remind myself. I was only defending my grandma. She'll attest to that. I want to leave as much intact as I can, and tell as much of the truth as I can. We haven't done anything wrong here.

Right?

I head back to the kitchen table. I zip up the duffel bag and sling the strap over my shoulder.

"You can't take that," my grandma says. "That's evidence."

"Evidence of what? All I know is some crazy people showed up to the motel and everything went to hell."

"And what do you think you're going to do with all that money?"

I look over my shoulder, through the living room doorway where I can faintly see Jasper's bare feet in the dark.

"I'm gonna do the right thing," I say. "For once in my life."

The sliding glass door is still open, letting in icy bursts of air from outside. I extend my elbow to my grandma, waiting for her to join me.

"Ready?"

She holds on to me as we go outside, crossing the icy parking lot back to our room.

"So what's the story, then?" she asks.

"We're going to tell the truth, obviously," I say. "To the police, I mean."

"Well, of course."

"But we're not mentioning this money to anyone. We don't need to mention anything we had no reason to know."

"Lana…"

"He wants me to make sure this gets to his girlfriend, and I'm gonna do that."

My grandma assumes I'm taking it all for myself, and I don't entirely blame her. I've lived my life thus far as a petty opportunist. Even still, I already have several bundles of cash stashed inside my luggage, after all. Which I'm keeping.

Once we make it back to our room, I stuff the entire duffel bag inside my luggage. I have to make a bit of a nest for it, pushing all my clothes to the sides to make room. Then I zip my luggage shut. It's a super tight, awkward fit, but it works.

"You still have your things packed and ready to go?" I ask.

My grandma's already waiting by the door with the handle of her luggage grasped firmly. I assist her to the truck, where I unlock the passenger door and help her to climb inside. It's a bit of a step. Then I place both of our luggage bags into the truck bed, climb into the driver's seat, and slam the door shut, sealing us into the muffled quiet.

"Start the engine," my grandma says. "It's freezing."

I do just that. The truck roars to life. I flip on the head-lights. Then I buckle in, pull us out, and take us to the road. This massive thing handles so much better in the snow than my car, which I can already see in the distance, its lonesome shape tipped into the ditch at the side of the road.

"Oh my goodness," my grandma says, spotting it herself. "You didn't make it very far…"

"No, I did not," I say, as I ease my foot onto the brake, slowing us down to a stop beside my wrecked vehicle.

"What are you doing? Why are we stopping?"

I don't answer as I quickly hop out of the truck and scamper around to my car. I reach inside, grab as many of the loose candies as I can, still sitting in the cup holders between the seats. I take them back with me, climbing slop-pily into the truck with my arms full. I dump them onto the long seat between my grandma and I before slamming my door shut and re-buckling my seatbelt.

I turn to see my grandma's unamused face as she looks between the candy and me, furrowing her brow in disap-pointment. I know she's wondering what the hell is wrong with me. I lean across the seat and plant a kiss on her wrin-kled cheek. She grimaces, but as I settle back into my seat I see the ghost of a smile she can't resist.

I adjust the rearview mirror and catch another glimpse of that red sign behind us, glowing bright and ominous onto the white-packed road. Then I rip open a candy for myself and tear a great big piece off with my teeth, as I drive us into the darkness ahead.

LANA

*a*fter passing through the town of Hodgerton, I use my newly restored cell signal and GPS to take us directly to the police station in Morgan, the next town over, where we report the night's horrid events and give each of our statements as accurately and honestly as possible—with the simple omission of any mention of the duffel bag stashed inside my luggage.

They hold us at the station for a time, until the police are kind enough to escort us to another nearby motel, where we're asked to stay until the following day, should there be any followup questions after they've conducted their survey of the crime scene. It's not like we can go anywhere, anyway, seeing as my car is stranded so many miles away and needs to be towed.

"Oh my *lordy*," my grandma says as we finally shut the door of our new motel room. It's much cleaner in appearance than the last, with newer furnishings and fresher paint on the walls.

My nose still hurts. I examine it in the bathroom mirror,

swollen and red around the bridge. I think it might actually be broken. I borrow some of my grandma's ibuprofen for the pain, at least. The knick on my forehead feels worse than it looks, where the bullet grazed me. Otherwise I think I'm okay.

I'm okay. We're okay.

Stepping out of the bathroom, I find my grandma standing by her new bed gently massaging her throat.

"You okay?" I ask.

She appears distracted as she looks up at me. "Oh yes, I'm fine. What about you?"

I nod in reply. Truthfully I could use another smoke before bed, but I decide the two I've had are enough for one night. I'd hate for this trip to turn me into a chain smoker after I've made so many attempts at quitting already.

"So," my grandma says. "In the morning…"

"I'll have my car towed to the nearest place," I say, already thinking well ahead for once. "Probably replace the airbags and the tires and…"

"And I'm paying for it," my grandma says. "No questions. I don't want you touching any of that money."

"I wasn't planning on it, Grandma."

I was, though. I absolutely was. And I still am, too. Later, of course. I'm not going to start spending any of it anytime soon, and I'm not going to spend it recklessly. I'll be smart. Or I'll try to be, anyway.

I take a seat on my bed, pull my phone from my pocket, and open up Jennifer's contact. It's way too late to bother her now, I think. I'll wait until the morning.

For now, I'm dying to get some sleep.

I dream of sleazy motels, savage storms, and struggling mothers.

I wake with tense hands, an imaginary tire iron gripped.

Images of blood and death are etched across the dark.

I close my eyes once more... and choose dreaming instead.

We're awakened by loud knocking on our motel room door. It's early enough that the morning light through the window is pale blue. All I can do is groan. Luckily my grandma—who operates on five hours of sleep most nights anyway—is up on her feet in an instant to answer the door.

The police are nice enough to bring us breakfast, at least, which makes getting out of bed a little easier. They also bring with them an avalanche of new questions regarding last night, now they've combed through the various crime scenes themselves. By the end of their questioning, I've basically given them an entire retelling of what happened. I also learn that Quentin's partner, Allen, was murdered in their room. I sorta figured as much. This news makes my grandma emotional for some reason, as if he was such a nice guy. Maybe he was, I don't know. My grandma also cries at Lifetime movies, though, so it's not too surprising.

She's still wiping tears from her eyes as the police leave.

"Are you okay, Grandma?"

"Oh, I don't know what I'm crying about," she says, as she enters the bathroom and blows her nose with toilet paper. She comes back out and forces a smile. "I think I'm still just tired, is all. I didn't sleep very well."

Understandable. I woke up multiple times myself, never getting more than an hour of sleep in between. We have a long day ahead of us, I know. Maybe a couple long days, depending on how long it takes to get my car figured out.

"We should find ourselves a car rental this morning," my grandma says. "We're not far from Franklin. We can finish our trip while your car gets fixed."

"Oh, yeah. I didn't even think of that."

Probably it didn't occur to me because I know I can't afford it. Well... not yet, anyway. Not until all this cop stuff is behind us.

Sitting on my bed with a breakfast burrito wrapper in my lap, I grab my phone from off the nightstand. I pull up her contact again. *Jennifer.* I'd like to get this over with, so I can finally stop thinking about it. Also...

"She has no idea," I mutter under my breath.

"Hmm?" my grandma says. "Did you say something?"

"She has no idea he's dead."

I hesitate with my phone in my hands, not sure what I should say, or how I should say it. I suppose I should start with the obvious. One step at a time.

My first text reads: *Is this Jennifer?*

We're parked outside of a closed-down shopping mall, the sprawling lot completely empty, plenty of space to see anyone coming, anyone going. The sky is overcast, an oppressive gray. But it isn't snowing. It hasn't snowed at all today, though there's plenty on the ground after last night.

Our rental car is an SUV with all-wheel drive, my grandma's choosing. She says we should have rented a car from the very beginning instead of taking mine, and I think she's right.

Hindsight and all the rest.

Another car pulls into the lot behind us. A brown sedan. I watch in the rearview as it comes, giving us a wide berth as it pulls around in a large circle. I see her behind the wheel. *Jennifer.* It's just her, as far as I can tell. She looks right back at me as she circles, confirming that it's just us as well—me and my elderly companion. I can't blame her. After the text conversation we had, I'd be wary as hell, too.

"There she is," my grandma says with a cheery lilt, like we're meeting a friend for lunch.

Jennifer stops beside us, the distance of one parking spot between our vehicles—we can't see the actual parking spots for all the snow. She starts climbing out, so I do the same, first reaching into the backseat and grabbing the duffel bag I brought with us. I step out into the crunchy snow to meet her there.

I really don't know what to expect.

She's even more beautiful in person than in the photo on Jasper's phone. I wish I could have given his phone to her, but I'd believed it to be a bad idea at the time—what with phones being so easily traceable. I think that's the last thing she needs.

As we stand apart, she looks at the bag I'm holding, her eyes never leaving it. She's been crying, I can tell. A lot. Her eyes are puffy and red.

She doesn't take them off the duffel bag as she says, "You were there when it happened?"

She means when her lover died, of course.

"Yeah. Yes. I was." I clear my throat. "So was my grandma. He, um… he saved her life."

Jennifer's eyes jump from the duffel bag to the window behind me, where she can see my grandma sitting in the passenger seat. There isn't much emotion in her eyes right now, despite the evidence of all the recent emotion she's displayed. She licks her lips, then presses them, like she's thinking really hard about something. Whatever thoughts she's turning over in her head, I don't think they're kind. Maybe she blames us? I've already told her everything over the phone. Everything I thought she needed to know, anyway. She knows even more than us, I'm sure. She actually knew Jasper, for starters.

We stand in silence for a prolonged moment, and it's only now I realize she's struggling not to fall apart before my very eyes. When she speaks again, her voice is thick, and fresh tears spill down her cheeks.

"I'm carrying his child."

She hangs her head, gazing upon her own belly, hidden under her coat. My own belly twists itself into knots as she says it.

"I'm so sorry."

I don't know what else to say. I don't think she wants my condolences. I don't think she *needs* my condolences. Without looking me in the eye, she steps forward and reaches to accept the bag.

So give it to her already.

I know I should just hand it over. I know I should just let

her go. I know that's all she wants, but instead I hesitate, feeling like I need to say something, something to make it better when obviously nothing will. Maybe I'm simply projecting, thinking that I'd want someone to reassure me if I were in her shoes.

I am in her shoes. Sort of...

I knew Jasper for an hour before his death. This woman doesn't need anything from me but the bag in my hands. But I see the fear in her eyes, and I feel a bit of the ache in her chest, too. I know that feeling. I know how it feels to lose the most important person in your world. I guess the silver lining here is that she was spared the grisly details. At least she didn't have to see...

And then it hits me.

"He was smiling," I say. "Like he was thinking about something really good just before he... you know. Like he was happy. I just... thought maybe you should know that."

I hand over the bag. She takes it into her arms, cradling it somberly how I imagine she'll someday cradle her newborn baby.

She snorts back her tears. "Thanks."

Then she looks at me. *Really* looks at me. Her eyes are glistening and raw. I see a million different thoughts in those eyes, all of them painful and frightened. Like how she'll never see him again, unable to even attend his funeral, if there will even be one. Whatever he had to do to obtain that money—whatever resulted in two armed thugs tracking him down to get it back—likely means she won't be returning home any time soon. She's on the run now, too, perhaps destined for a life of sleazy motels and always looking over her shoulder. Until she gets away, anyway. I hope she gets away.

I hope this life doesn't follow her to the ends of the earth.

She turns and climbs back into her car without another word. She's left it running, a steady cloud of exhaust pluming into the air all the while. She departs without even a second glance.

I climb back into the rental, glad that it's over, glad that it's out of my hands.

"Poor girl," my grandma says as I settle in behind the wheel.

"She'll be okay," I say, as if I have any idea.

She has to be.

As I buckle my seatbelt, my grandma catches my hand in both of hers. She gives the back of my hand a quick kiss, followed by a comforting rub between her smooth-but-papery ones. She smiles at me in that knowing way only she can pull off so well.

"I think so, too," she says.

DARLENE

EPILOGUE

*F*ranklin is just how I remember it. There are differences, sure. Old establishments have closed and reopened as new ones. More apartments and condos have sprouted up where there used to be empty space. But it *feels* the same, and that's what matters. That's what makes coming back so magical. This is where I grew up, where my life began, where my life was shaped into what it would become even when I put this place behind me.

This is where I met the love of my life.

Lana follows my directions without question, without complaint, as I lead us through endless detours, pointing out all the places I still remember—where her grandfather and I went on dates, where I got into my first fender-bender, where I worked my first job bagging groceries.

It's lovely being back. My memories of this place are so much stronger, so much more vivid, than recent ones. Because these memories were formative. They're my foundation. They're not going anywhere. If they do, I'm not me anymore.

The second-to-last stop is my childhood home. It's changed as much as anything else. It's been repainted. Trees have been cut down. The lawn has been xeriscaped. The detached garage appears to have been converted into an apartment of sorts.

"There used to be a great big walnut tree here," I tell Lana, as she leans toward my window to see the place from the curb. "Your mother... when she was little, she loved coming outside and collecting them off the ground. We'd fill buckets."

"My mom was here?" Lana says.

I realize I've let something slip. It's not necessarily a secret, but the story isn't one I'm fond of telling. I suppose Lana deserves to know these things, however. Her mother's past is her past, too, in a way.

"Have I never told you?" I say, playing dumb. "I brought your mom here for a little while. When things weren't so good between your grandfather and me."

"Oh. Yeah, I had no idea. How long?"

"We were separated about a year."

"A year?"

I shrug, then sigh. "Give or take. But it was for the best. Absence makes the heart grow fonder, as they say..."

I turn to my granddaughter and find her staring down the street, her mind connecting dots in faraway places I can't even begin to guess.

"How old was she?"

I have to think about it. "I believe your mom was about... eight or nine, the first time."

"The first time?"

"She was about fourteen the second time."

"You and grandpa separated twice?"

A sigh again, bigger and more dramatic than the first.

"We were stupid. We didn't know how to communicate about anything. Every little disagreement turned into a big one. Then resentment. We mostly figured it out the second time, though."

Lana continues staring into the distance, though she narrows her eyes in thought.

"Huh. I don't think my mom ever mentioned that."

It's beginning to dawn on me now, where Lana's head is at.

"I think that's when your mother's troubles started. When she started acting out. I can't say for certain whether it was the separations themselves, or rather... the periods that *led up to* the separations. Because those were messy. Your mom saw and heard a lot of things I wish she hadn't. We were practically children ourselves. I don't mean to make excuses, of course, I just... have a lot of regrets, is all. Sometimes I wonder: *if I'd done this differently, or that differently, maybe she'd have turned out differently, too, or maybe she wouldn't have struggled so much.* I felt so... *helpless*, to help her in any meaningful way. I tried, but it was like everything just spiraled out of my control, like the damage was already done and there was nothing I could do for her. And then... after her accident, you know... I beat myself up plenty."

I realize I'm rambling, that I'm talking about myself too much, defending myself too much, when that's not necessarily what Lana is asking for, what she's needing right now.

"What are you thinking?" I ask, as her silence is driving me crazy at this point.

"Nothing," she says. That one word weighs heavy on my heart. "I just never knew much about her childhood, I guess."

I'm not sure what else to say. I'm not as wise as my years would suggest. When nothing comes to me in a timely manner, and Lana doesn't appear to have anything else to say or ask, I decide to change the subject altogether.

"Well, how about we head to our last stop? I think we're both ready to start winding down this adventure, hmm?"

Lana pulls away from the curb without another word. Though, as I steal glances while she drives, I can tell she's still thinking. Still dwelling.

Something else on her mind.

Eventually we arrive at our final destination. The sky is still overcast, and the sprawling pond before us is thoroughly frozen, freshly blanketed with last night's snowfall. Lana shuts off the engine but neither of us budge for a minute or two, simply staring out over the park. She hasn't spoken much since we left my childhood home. I haven't said much, either, as I thought it best to give her time and space to process whatever's eating at her. I'm not exactly sure what it is, though there are a few obvious possibilities.

"Well," I say. "Shall we?"

I decide to lead the charge, climbing out of the car with my husband's silver urn already in hand. I slam the door shut. Then I stand and listen. It's quiet. Everything's muffled from the snow. The air is clean and crisp in my lungs, on my tongue.

I make my way down the slope toward the edge of the pond. Lana follows behind me, our boots crunching. I turn to her as she sidles up beside me, and I'm pleased to see she gives me half a smile. It's forced for my sake, but that means something in and of itself. I peer across the pond, toward the dark thickets on the other side. There's nobody here but us, which surprises me.

"When I was younger… *much* younger… this place would be full of kids on a day like this. This was prime ice skating territory."

"Is this where you and grandpa met?" Lana asks.

"It is!" I say, surprised that she guessed it. "Though, it was during the summer. I was seventeen. He was nineteen…"

"If you met in the summer, why'd we come out here *now*?"

"Well, because we *came back,* of course. Several times. We met here, sure, but we spent a lot of time here together otherwise."

"Did you ice skate together, too? Like a scene straight out of some corny Lifetime movie?"

"No, we never ice skated. But we did build a snowman once. We also had picnics. We came here during all the seasons."

"Did you move to Florida because you were sick of the snow?"

"No," I say with a laugh. Though my humor quickly

withers as the answer reaches my mouth. "We left because we both felt we needed to get away from this place. From our parents. All of it. And then we had your mom. I was such a clueless mother... and wife... anytime something went wrong, I came running right back."

Lana goes quiet again. No followup questions. I glance her way and spy her staring into the distance, into those black-brown thickets across the pond, mulling over whatever she's been mulling over all morning.

"Do I remind you of her?" she says suddenly. It's not what I expect to come out of my granddaughter's mouth. "Of my mom, I mean..."

"Well, of course you do," I say. "How could you not?"

Lana sucks in her lip, chewing it in thought—and possibly working overtime to suppress the emotions her eyes betray.

"How much, though?" she says, and by this point her eyes are sparkling.

"Oh, Lana..." I set the urn in the snow and throw my arms around her, as I can clearly see she's struggling to hold herself together on her own. "You remind me of your mother in all the best ways. *Only* the best ways."

"I..." Lana chokes on her words. The sound of her voice only makes me squeeze her that much harder. "Grandma... I'm pregnant."

Her words hit me like a ton of bricks. I'm hardly able to believe my ears. I release her then, only so that I can get a better look at her.

"Pregnant?"

Tears stream down her cheeks. She can't look me in the eye, instead looking across the frozen pond, her mouth twisted up too much to speak, but she nods in confirmation. I pull her against myself again, squeeze her even tighter than before.

"Oh, sweetheart…"

"I don't want to be like her," she says, her words muddied through the sobs. "I don't want her life. I… I don't…"

She's positively *trembling* in the cold. But I don't think the cold is even half of it.

"Oh, sweetheart," I repeat. It's all I can say at first. It's a moment before my better wisdom reaches through the shock. "We'll figure this out together, okay? Don't you worry. We'll figure this out."

"I can't even take care of myself," she says. Her voice is reedy. Barely understandable. *"I can't do this…"*

"You can do *anything*," I tell her. The words leave my mouth impulsively. Unthinkingly. I realize I'm all she's got right now. She needs more than meaningless platitudes. "Whatever you decide, sweetheart… whatever you decide, I'll support you, all right? I'm not going anywhere." I can't help glancing toward the urn in the snow at our feet. A grim reminder. I push those thoughts aside. "Just trust yourself, okay? I'll be right there with you every step of the way, whichever way that might be…"

"I don't want you to be disappointed in me…"

My poor heart can hardly withstand the sound of her voice.

"I'm not disappointed in you!" I say. I rub her back aggressively, like I can stop her trembling with friction alone. "What's there to be disappointed about? I just want you to be happy, Lana. That's all I want."

I pull away from her again, holding her at arm's length, and I'm relieved to find she can look me in the eye now, though hers are still so wet.

"We'll figure this out. Do you understand? It's going to be okay. Everything is going to be okay."

She actually smiles now. *Smiles!* Even as her cheeks are still wet. Those tears will be frozen to her face in another few seconds. I wipe them away. Then I pull her against myself for one last squeeze. When I release her again, it seems the worst of the storm has passed.

"Okay," she says, and finishes wiping her own eyes dry. She clears her throat. "Sorry. I'm done now. Promise…"

"Nothing to be sorry for," I say. "We'll talk about this more later, all right? We have a lot more driving ahead of us, after all." I bend and grab the urn. Hopefully my husband doesn't mind me setting him on the ground for a moment or two, wherever he is. "All right, well… what say we move this party along, hmm?"

Lana smiles again. A weak one. There's a laugh in there somewhere, too, I just know it.

"Where are you scattering them?" she says. "Aren't you supposed to do it in the water?"

"I was thinking about dumping them in the snow."

Lana looks at me funny. "The snow?"

"I thought we could build a snowman, maybe. Build it right on the ice. Then he'll end up in the pond eventually. When it melts."

Lana considers this. She sniffles a bit.

"Okay, that's not a bad idea."

"Or we could dump his ashes in the snow and have ourselves a snowball fight."

She looks at me like I've lost my marbles.

"You don't like that?" I say. "You don't think it'd be funny if I pelted you in the head with grandpa?"

She lets it out then—the laugh I knew she had in her. It warms me, that laugh. Just like her mother's.

"I like the snowman idea better," she says.

"Well, all right, then," I say. "A snowman it is."

I uncap the urn, turn the ashes onto the cold snow, and we get to finishing what we started.

A SPECIAL THANKS

Dear brave reader,

I must say thank you. Without readers like you, authors like me wouldn't be allowed a paddle in this violent, ever-changing sea—otherwise known as the publishing world.

I only write these twisted, twisty stories with the utmost love and sincerity, so to be granted your curiosity means more than you can ever know.

If you have a moment, let me know your thoughts by leaving a review. It's a simple gesture that means the world to us indie publishers and helps other curious readers like yourself find books like mine. I'd greatly appreciate it.

Thanks again! There are plenty more thrills to come!

With love,
Beau

Made in the USA
Columbia, SC
30 January 2025